I STILL DO

MELANIE D. SNITKER

DALLIONI MEDIA, LLC

I Still Do
(Healing Hearts Series)

© 2018 Melanie D. Snitker

Published by
Dallionz Media, LLC
P.O. Box 643
Boerne, TX 78006

Cover Design: Blue Valley Author Services
Editor: Krista Burdine - Grammaresque

For permission requests, please contact the author at the e-mail below or through her website.

Melanie D. Snitker
melanie@melaniedsnitker.com
www.melaniedsnitker.com

Praise God for the ultimate second chance.

For God so loved the world that he
gave his one and only son,
that whoever believes in him
shall not perish but have eternal life.
John 3:16 (NIV)

CHAPTER ONE

C ora Wells filled the last of the four vials of blood she was taking from her patient. After she set the vial on the nearby tray, she carefully taped the small catheter against the older woman's arm to secure it for use as a future IV. "There we go, Mrs. Sayles. See, that didn't hurt too much, did it?"

Karen Sayles gingerly pressed the tape as though she were afraid it would come loose. "Well, it did hurt, but it was better than I expected. At least you didn't use a square needle this time." Her eyes sparkled with humor.

Cora chuckled. "I should hope not. Where did someone use a square needle?"

"The lab on Main. My arm was bruised for a week."

Cora finished putting her patient's ID stickers on each of the tubes of blood before regarding her with a sympathetic look. "That's not good. Hopefully that tech's skills have improved drastically since then."

Mrs. Sayles nodded. She pointed to one of the pockets of Cora's scrubs. "That's a beautiful pin."

Cora's hand brushed the metal angel that she always kept

pinned to her scrubs. "Thank you. It reminds me that God sends us help when we need it, even if it's not always the way we expect." She never hesitated to tell her patients the true meaning of the pin she wore, but she also found out that not many people asked about it unless they had similar beliefs.

"That's a lovely thought," Mrs. Sayles said as she leaned her head against the hospital bed. The poor woman had come into Denton Regional Hospital's emergency room with several unusual symptoms, including intense pain in her lower back. Upon initial examination by Dr. Coalson, the cause was uncertain. He'd ordered blood work and, because of Mrs. Sayles' high blood pressure and heart rate, a bag of saline to make sure she was properly hydrated.

Cora patted the older woman on the hand. "I'm going to take these to the lab. I'll be back to get you hooked up with some fluids to help you feel a little better."

"That sounds good. Any chance you could add a little painkiller to those fluids?"

Mrs. Sayles had indicated a high pain level when she was first brought into the ER. Cora smiled kindly. "I'll check with the doctor for you." She moved the control within reach. "Remember, just push that green button if you need me for anything. I won't be long." With a last comforting smile, she left the small triage room.

After making sure the blood was delivered to the lab, Cora tucked a wayward blond lock behind one ear and headed for the nurse's station at the center of the ER. She'd French-braided her long hair first thing that morning and used some bobby pins and hair spray to preserve the hairstyle for as long as she could. Her hair was so straight and fine, though, that it always managed to escape at some point during the day. As her coworker, and fellow nurse, Jen, would say, it was a good problem to have. Especially compared to Jen's curly hair that often turned frizzy.

Jen handed Cora a steaming mug filled with coffee from the coffee maker in the break room. Cora took one sip and tried not to grimace. "George must've made it this morning."

Jen nodded. "Yep. Someone needs to teach that man how to make a real cup of coffee." She took a tentative sip from her own before pushing it away. "That's not going to happen. The vending machine it is. You want anything?" When Cora shook her head, Jen stood. She patted her curly hair with a frown. "I really wish it weren't so muggy today."

Cora doubted her friend would mind the warmer weather so much if her hair didn't take on a permanently frizzy look in the heat.

"Okay, I'll be right back." Within five minutes, she'd returned with a can of Dr Pepper. She sat down again before opening it and taking a swig. "It's going to be so strange not seeing you on Friday. I swear, you're practically always on shift. I don't think I've ever seen you take an unscheduled day off."

That was an exaggeration, but not a huge one. It was true Cora took as many shifts as she could safely work. She liked to think of it as dedication as opposed to not having enough of a life like Jen often accused her of. Well, that and a need for money to pay for her apartment and insurance. She may not have grown up knowing she wanted to be registered nurse, but now she knew this was totally her calling. "It will be weird. But I'll be back to work again on Monday."

Cora spotted Dr. Coalson come around the corner. She flagged him down and told him of Mrs. Sayles' request for pain medication. The doctor agreed and wrote orders on the patient's chart.

"As soon as we get that blood work back, I'll come in and

speak with her again."

Cora nodded. "I'll let her know." She looked at Jen. "I'm sure you all will get along just fine without me."

"Maybe so, but I can't help but wish I were going with you. Aspen, Colorado would be an amazing change from all of our heat and humidity."

Jen frequently made it clear how much she disliked the warm summers in Texas. According to her, it was practically a sin for the temperatures to remain above sixty into the second week of November. It seemed as though fall was nearly non-existent this year. While Cora sometimes missed the pretty autumns she'd seen in other locations, she didn't miss the nasty winter weather. As far as she was concerned, it was a good trade-off.

"Cooler weather would be nice. I plan on curling up by a roaring fire while reading a good book." Cora smiled. She'd told Jen about the trip a while ago but kept the details to a minimum.

"Well, you should definitely get out a little. Learn how to ski. Something."

"I promise I won't stay a hermit the entire time," Cora said with a smile.

"Good. I'm going to hold you to that. It's a free vacation, and you need to take advantage of that. So, tell me about your ex-husband's family. You must've been close if you were invited." Curiosity shone in Jen's eyes.

Cora resisted the urge to sigh. It always seemed to baffle Jen that Cora didn't want to spill about her personal life. Especially when Cora probably knew more about Jen and her family than she'd ever wanted to know.

Besides, just thinking about Grey Jackson had Cora's heart aching. "I spent most of my time with his family through high school. There's Grey, his younger brother, Dare, and his older brother, Flynn. I guess their dad took off before Dare was born, and Flynn always kind of filled in the protector role. He never did like me. My parents were so messed up, and Grey's mom and grandfather kind of took me under their wings…" Her voice caught. She'd spent a lot of time visiting with Grandpa Jackson. It was still hard to believe he was gone.

She'd attended his funeral several months ago and stayed at the back of the church. Other than saying hello to Grey's mom, Maria Jackson, she hadn't really spoken to anyone else. She'd watched Grey from a distance as he grieved with his family but didn't think he realized she'd attended at all. Which was probably for the best. Grandpa Jackson's funeral was not the place to reopen old wounds.

"I guess this is some sort of gathering to remember his grandfather. Some kind of last wish. I wouldn't even consider attending except that Grandpa Jackson included me in the list of people he wanted to invite before he died, and I respected the guy too much to turn the invitation down." Not to say she hadn't regretted her decision to go at least a dozen times. She might have escaped the funeral without facing Grey, but it was highly unlikely she'd be able to do the same when they were all in a big cabin together in the mountains.

She shrugged as though it were no big deal. Truthfully, it'd touched her heart more than she could say to have Grandpa Jackson remember her like that. As much as she dreaded seeing Grey or dealing with Flynn's disapproving stares, she did want to honor Grandpa Jackson's memory.

She still wondered what possessed him to plan such an interesting event in his final weeks. Attending this reunion would be anything but easy, though.

Jen touched her arm. "It sounds like he was a really nice man."

"Yeah, he was."

"How long has it been since you've seen your ex?"

Cora forced a casual smile. She hadn't spoken to Grey since they'd signed the final divorce papers over five years ago. "Probably not long enough." They laughed, although Cora really felt like crying. Or drowning the memories in a big bowl of chocolate ice cream.

Grey and his family lived in San Antonio. She'd moved to the Dallas area shortly after their divorce and now lived in Denton. Texas was a big state, but she supposed it was inevitable that they'd run into each other again. She never would've guessed it'd be in Colorado, though.

She wondered if Grey had changed much. Had he attended the funeral with another woman? Cora went over everything in her mind and didn't remember seeing anyone. That meant nothing, though. He was probably remarried now, and his wife was somewhere watching over their kids. For the first time, she regretted not keeping track of him over the years. She'd considered checking up on him several times but decided that it wouldn't do her any good. She'd needed a clean break back then, and time didn't change that.

Still, it would be nice if she knew exactly what she was getting into this weekend. Pushing that thought away, she chose to focus on her job. She might not be able to do anything about her own painful past, but she could at least lessen her patient's discomfort.

GREY JACKSON SIGHED as he went over his list of things to accomplish by the end of the day. He knew his manager, Brody, could handle everything while he was gone. At the end of the day, though, Defending Yesterday was something he'd built from the ground up, and it wasn't a secret how much the store meant to him.

He'd worked for his mom and grandfather in their family's antique shop in San Antonio since he was in high school, traveling frequently in search of collectibles for them to sell. Once he'd saved up his own money, he'd opened a shop of his own in Fort Worth. Flynn, eight years Grey's senior, had been less than happy about Grey moving away from home instead of continuing to help Mom and Grandpa run the family business. Grey had to get out of San Antonio, though, for a variety of reasons. He hated that it'd put strain on his relationship with Flynn, but he'd never regretted his decision.

While Mom and Grandpa focused on household antiques and kitchen collectibles, Grey was more interested in modern as well as antique guns, knives, and anything that could be used camping, hiking, or in survival situations. Those first few months after the store opened were slow until word got around that Defending Yesterday often had items that couldn't be found elsewhere.

The bell over the door rang as a customer came into the store. Grey recognized Abe, a long-time customer who had been coming to the store since it first opened. "Hey, good to see you, man." They shook hands. "I've got it right over here."

Abe's eyes danced with excitement as he rubbed his hands together. "I appreciate the call. I've been looking for one of these for years."

"Not a problem." Grey unlocked the glass case where he displayed the handguns he had for sale. As his hand closed around the Colt 1911, he was instantly aware of the history that he held in his palm. He'd only seen the classic from World War II once or twice before. It was also exactly what Abe had been looking for.

He demonstrated the gun was unloaded before handing it over to Abe.

"She is a beauty." Abe took his time inspecting the gun, but there was no doubt he was happy with it. "You don't see one of these every day."

"No, sir, you sure don't." It'd cost Grey a lot when he'd traded for it earlier that week, but he knew he'd make his money back and then some. Deals like this were what he thrived on.

Abe examined it for several more minutes before nodding definitely. "I'll take her."

Grey grinned. "Fantastic. Okay, let me get the paperwork. While you fill that out, I'll get everything together for you."

He carefully packaged the gun in a plastic gun case. After getting payment squared away and allowing Abe to inspect the gun and agree that all was present, Grey reached for one of the plastic bags he had hanging up next to a sign that read, "Prayer is the most powerful weapon in your arsenal." He handed the bag over. "It was great doing business with you, Abe. You'll have to come back and let me know how it shoots."

"You've got it, Grey." They shook hands. "You have a good day."

"Yep, you, too."

The door closed behind Abe as Brody, the store's manager, walked up. "Impressive sale, Boss Man. It kinda hurts to see that gun leave."

"That it does." If it hadn't been for the high price tag, Grey would've kept the gun for himself. "I think that was the last thing I had hoped to get accomplished today. You sure you don't mind if I leave early?"

"Nah, I've got it all under control."

"Great. Remember, if you guys need anything, feel free to

call. I'm not sure what kind of reception I'll have at the cabin. They're predicting a blizzard, so getting in touch may be tricky. I'll try to check messages frequently."

"Don't worry about it, Boss Man. We've got this," Brody said, his voice tinged with amusement. "Like I said, if there's a problem I can't handle, I'll call you. Meanwhile, enjoy getting away for a while. And try not to break a leg on those ski slopes, huh?"

Grey chuckled. "Yeah, I'll do that."

There was a time when he was constantly traveling around the country in search of items to bring into his store. Now, he mostly left that up to Brody or waited for things to come through his door. Even though he didn't travel often, he was certainly no stranger to packing for a road trip.

This one to Colorado, though, was full of the unknown. Sure, Grey had been to Aspen several times growing up when his family went for vacation. He needed warm clothes and all his winter gear. But it wasn't the cold weather or the snow he didn't know how to prepare for.

There were a lot of things that he and his older brother, Flynn, didn't see eye to eye on, and Cora was at the center of that. Normally visits were short and sweet. The idea of being in the same house as Flynn for an entire weekend made Grey cringe.

As far as Flynn was concerned, Cora had never been good enough to marry into the family. The fact that she was poor and had no real familial ties of her own automatically made her a gold digger. It wasn't that Grey's family was particularly wealthy: His father walked out before Dare was born, and their mother struggled to provide for her three sons along with Grandpa's help. Because of that, Flynn was protective of the money that they had worked hard to accumulate. Flynn was confident Cora only wanted someone to provide for her monetarily, and he never did let that go. Especially when Grey agreed to give Cora half of everything when they got divorced.

The best Grey could figure was that Flynn equated Cora leaving with half the money to their father walking out on the family. Their situation wasn't even remotely similar, but Flynn never would listen to reason.

This weekend wasn't going to be easy on several different levels.

Mom was looking forward to this trip and finally getting all three of her sons together again under one roof. He didn't want to disappoint her, and he really didn't want to get in a fight with Flynn over the weekend. It was more than that, though. He'd be seeing Cora again.

She was the woman he'd loved since high school. The woman he'd married and thought would be a part of his life forever. The two years following their wedding had been some of the most amazing, painful, and confusing of his life. Ultimately, he'd lost her, and he'd had to learn how to rebuild his life.

He hadn't spoken to her in years. There was no way he could adequately come up with a list to cover all the scenarios that might possibly crop up over this weekend.

When he'd first found out about the trip his grandfather had put in his will, Grey had been shocked. Sure, Grandpa talked about a trip to reunite their family and get them talking again, but Grey had thought it was just the musings of a senti-mental old man. A man who often spoke about how much Aspen meant to him. If Grey heard the story once about how Grandpa and Grandma had met there, he'd heard it a million times. It always made Grey smile. In fact, Aspen was where his grandparents married only months after that first meeting.

Grandpa had put in his will that his last wish was for the

family to gather at the large cabin in Aspen for his birthday. How was Grey—or anyone else—supposed to say no to that? Grandpa always had said it was better to face your problems than run away from them. Grey suspected this was Grandpa's way of making them all do that.

It was some time later before Grey discovered that Grandpa had included Cora on the invitation list. Grey shouldn't have been surprised. Cora was at his family's house nearly as often as he was through high school. Grandpa had seen the hurt Cora experienced growing up and knew that she needed someone to play the grandparent figure in her life. With her own family highly dysfunctional, and bordering on abusive at times, Cora spent as much time away from her own home as possible.

Cora and Grandpa had become close. So, when Grey spotted Cora at the funeral in San Antonio months ago, hanging out at the back of the church, it felt right for her to be there. But his heart had still leapt in his chest, and all the amazing memories that included her, collided with the painful ones.

He'd given her space during the funeral and never spoke to her, which was probably for the best. Except now he thought it might have been easier if that first conversation— no matter how brief or awkward—was already behind them.

They were going to be in the same cabin together for the weekend. Throw in Flynn, who he figured was probably livid that she'd been included, and it was not a good combination. It was unlikely he and Cora could avoid each other forever. Not for the first time, he prayed they'd all make it through this reunion without fistfights. If for no other reason, to make Mom happy and honor Grandpa's memory.

CHAPTER TWO

C ora took in a deep breath the moment she stepped off the plane. She hated flying. No, she despised it. She'd only been on a plane twice before, but this flight was the worst. It was bad enough getting to the gate at the last moment before boarding. Add to it the horrible turbulence and the blizzard they could barely fly through, and Cora was a bundle of nerves.

As soon as she walked through the tunnel that led to the airport, she made a beeline for the restroom. The Aspen/Pitkin County Airport thrummed with activity. She heard people mention that her plane was the last one in until the blizzard cleared, and that many flights had been cancelled going out as well. It would be a real mess to sort through.

All Cora was hoping for at this point was that the cabin wasn't too far away, and that she could hire a taxi or rent a car to get her there before it became impossible to travel. She did not want to be stuck at the airport for the weekend.

Once she left the restroom, she located a sign telling her where to pick up her luggage and then headed for the counter to find some transportation. The smell of snow filled the area as the main revolving doors continued to bring in fresh, cold air.

For the tenth time that day, she wished she hadn't come. She patted the back pocket of her jeans where the ticket stub from her flight resided. Maybe it was silly, but the stub reminded her of how much Grandpa Jackson wanted her to be here today, and that's what had given her the courage she needed every step of the way.

Just thinking about him made her bottom lip quiver a little. She pulled it in between her teeth and steadied her emotions as she waited in the long line of people needing transportation. Her reason for being here alone was enough to make her cry over the loss of the only man who'd truly been a grandfather to her. There were enough difficult emotions involved seeing as how she was going to have to deal with Grey. The last thing she needed was for him to see her face all red and blotchy from crying.

No, Cora needed to hold it together. She had no idea what this weekend had in store and was determined to keep her reactions in check. She rolled her shoulders back and confidently awaited her turn. When she finally reached the counter, the grave look on the man's face there did little to offer encouragement.

"Can I help you?"

"Yes, I'm trying to get to this cabin…" She pulled out the information Maria had sent her and handed it to the man. "Is there a shuttle or anything like that?"

"I'm afraid not, miss. We've had to call them all in with this storm."

"Do you have cars for rent? Anything?" Cora's stomach sank. See, she should've gone with her gut and stayed home. As it was, she was going to be stuck at the airport and still not be part of this family reunion thing. At least at home, she'd be enjoying the seventy-degree weather and watching re-runs on TV.

The man gave her a map of the area, circled the cabin she was supposed to be staying in, and then gave her a map of the airport as well. "If you'll go here," he told her and circled that area, "you can speak to someone who's trying to find everyone here some kind of accommodation while we ride out this storm. With any luck, it won't be as bad as they've been predicting."

"Great. Thank you." It was impossible to keep the disappointment from her voice. She walked away from the counter, her carry-on bag over one shoulder, one hand on her rolling suitcase, and the other holding the map. A voice spoke from behind her that jolted her heart into overtime.

"Did I hear you need a ride?"

She knew that voice as well as she knew her own: Grey.

She turned slowly to find him watching her with curiosity. He was standing near the window, his luggage at his feet. He'd changed some, and yet everything about him was familiar from his strong jaw to the breadth of his shoulders.

She realized she was holding her breath. She'd known this moment was coming but hadn't expected it to be quite so soon.

"Um…yeah. Apparently, they're all out of, well, everything." That was smooth.

The corners of his mouth lifted into a little smile. "So I heard. The rest of the family got here yesterday. When they heard about the storm, Flynn came down here and reserved a truck for me with four-wheel-drive and snow tires just in case." He held up a set of keys. "Turns out it's a good thing he did."

"You're not joking." Flynn always had been quite the planner, to the point of being overly controlling. In fact, he

14

and Grey both did a lot of primitive camping and things like that together before they started growing apart. Grey often spoke about being prepared for any eventuality whenever possible. It was no surprise that Flynn had thought things through ahead of time, too.

"You're welcome to ride out there with me if you'd like." He glanced out the window at the swirling snow. "We'd better get going, though. The guy gave me the truck but cautioned against driving in this. I'm thinking the sooner we leave the better."

Ride in a truck, just her and Grey? Cora wished she had another choice. But she couldn't hide from Grey this weekend, and she certainly didn't want to sleep at the airport. Besides, speaking to him for the first time where the rest of the family wasn't watching was probably better, anyway. She'd rip that stinking bandage right off and be done with it.

Her decision made, she took a steadying breath and squared her shoulders. "That would be great, thank you."

"You're welcome. Come on, the lot is this way."

They fought their way through the crowds of people until they came to the door leading to the parking lot outside.

Grey put his heavy coat on and Cora followed suit. He turned to look at her then, and his green eyes—a color that had always made her think of a meadow just after a heavy rainfall—focused on her. "Here let me take your suitcase. Just follow me." Without waiting for her to respond, he picked hers up like it weighed nothing. Although that was Grey—always the gentleman.

Now that they were walking next to each other, Cora was reminded of just how much taller he was. She'd always felt tiny in comparison. His sandy brown hair, with subtle red highlights that probably still shone in the sun, looked much the same. Maybe cropped a little closer than he used to keep it.

He was still just as handsome as ever. That realization made Cora's heart stutter.

The attraction between them—the spark—had never gone away. At least not for her. It was more like everything else that had been wrong with their relationship had overpowered it.

It didn't matter, though. He could be remarried by now.

She glanced at his left hand. No wedding band. Then he probably had a steady girlfriend, or a fiancée. A whole lot could happen in five years.

Snow began to cover their jackets the moment they stepped outside. The snowflakes alone were shockingly cold as they hit Cora's skin. It was the howling wind, however, that really drove the freezing temperatures home.

It wasn't hard to find the rental truck since most of the lot was empty. Grey hit the clicker on the keys to unlock it, opened the passenger door for Cora, and then stowed their luggage in the back seat. "I'll be right there. I just want to get my pocket knife and boot knife out of my bag. They don't do me much good in there."

Once he found what he was looking for, he put the pocket knife where it belonged and then slipped the larger knife into his boot. Cora brushed the snow off her pants and jacket onto the floorboard as Grey got behind the wheel.

"Wow, that's a lot of snow." He leaned forward a little so he could look at the sky through the windshield.

Her eyes widened. "Do you think we should go back into the airport?"

"Do you want to weather the storm out there?"

He knew she disliked everything that had to do with

flying, including airports. Usually people say they like lift off. Or landings. Or at least the beauty of the view far below. Yeah, not Cora. There was nothing positive enough about the flight to outweigh the fact she was floating thousands of miles above the ground in a tin can crowded with way too many people.

"Nope."

"Me, neither." Grey started the engine, turned the windshield wipers and heater on full. "You still have that map the guy at the counter gave you?"

"Sure." Cora pulled it out of her bag. "I thought you'd been here a lot before."

"A lot is three or four times, and it's been years." He took the map from her and studied it a moment before handing it back. He glanced at her and then slowly made his way through the parking lot to the road. Or rather, what was a road before all the snow had buried it. "In the interest of full disclosure, this isn't going to be easy."

"Are you saying there's a chance we may not get to the cabin?"

He tapped the map and another cabin that was between them and the one the man had circled. "I'm saying we'll get to a cabin, I'm just hoping we can make it far enough to get to the right one." He flashed her a grin she knew full well meant he was ready for a challenge.

"Is this the point where I start praying fervently for our safety?"

"That certainly never hurts."

Fantastic.

She said a silent prayer that they'd get to their destination in one piece. Only then did she realize she'd been clenching the edge of the map hard enough to crumple the edges. "I wonder what Grandpa Jackson would say if he saw us now.

17

He'd probably either feel bad he dragged us all out into this or find it highly amusing."

Grey kept his eyes on the road in front of him. "As long as everyone was still safe, he'd probably consider this a grand adventure." He paused. "I take it you don't feel the same way."

She shrugged, although she wasn't sure he saw her. "I'm not sure I'd go that far."

"Well, Grandpa would've appreciated your sacrifice."

Cora's gaze snapped to his face, reacting instantly to his words. Was he being sarcastic? She'd do anything for Grandpa Jackson, and Grey knew it. If he insinuated anything different, she'd let him know just how wrong he was.

But there was nothing in his expression to suggest he was upset or making fun of her.

She forced herself to relax a little. "I loved Grandpa Jackson. If he wanted me to be here, I couldn't say no." Tears pricked the back of her eyelids, and she blinked them away. Grey was the last person she wanted to cry in front of. They'd been there, done that.

She hadn't seen Grandpa Jackson much after she and Grey got divorced. She'd spoken to him over the phone here and there, but it wasn't the same. That was something she'd always regret. While she may talk big about how she should've stayed home, the truth was, nothing would've kept her away from Aspen this weekend.

She wondered what Grey thought about her being here. Was he glad she'd done what his grandfather asked? Or had he hoped she'd decline so he wouldn't have to see her again?

The tires of the truck hit a pothole beneath the layer of snow, and the vehicle pulled hard to the right. Grey gripped the steering wheel with both hands as he maneuvered through a blanket of white. Cora stared out the window, trying to find something to tell her where they might be. The only thing she could really make out were trees, and they all looked alike.

"Please tell me you're having better luck following our route than I am," she said quietly.

At first, she didn't think he'd heard her at all. Several minutes later, he released a loud hiss of air as the truck tires hit something and the vehicle jerked to a stop. "This is only getting worse."

The snowfall? Or visibility? It didn't matter, because he was right on either count.

He reached for the map again and studied it. "I think we're probably about here." He pointed to a spot not far from the first cabin he'd joked about earlier. But there was nothing on his face to indicate he was teasing now. "At this point, I think we should get to that cabin and reevaluate the situation there."

Grey tried to get the truck to go forward, but the tires only spun in the snow. When he put it in reverse, the same thing happened. Cora groaned, but he maintained his cool as he pulled the hood of his coat on over his head and got out of the truck.

It felt like he was gone forever before he returned with a serious look on his face. "I'm going to cut down some pine branches and see if I can use them to get us some traction out of the hole back here." He closed the door and opened the back door of the truck. After going through his suitcase for a moment, he retrieved gloves and a hat.

Cora released her seatbelt and reached for the door handle. "I'll help."

"Did you bring gloves?"

"To Aspen in the middle of winter?" Okay, that came out harsher than she'd intended. "Yes, I brought gloves."

She leaned through the space between the two front seats

and opened the zippered front of her rolling suitcase. It only took a moment to locate her gloves and hat. She pulled them on, welcoming the added warmth.

Without another word, they went to work. Grey used his knife to cut down pine branches that he handed to Cora. Once they had enough, he put them in place and then motioned for her to get back into the truck.

Cora crossed her gloved fingers as he started the engine. It took several attempts, but he managed to get the truck out of the hole and moving forward again. "Woot! That was close."

"Yeah, too close."

Instead of the triumphant expression she expected to see on his face, his jaw was clenched as he focused on driving. A half hour later, a cabin appeared through the white blanket of snow falling in front of them.

There were no other cars visible and the windows were dark.

Cora expected Grey to continue on. Instead, he pulled in close to the cabin and turned the engine off.

"What are we doing?"

"We're going to have to wait out the storm here. We can find our way to the main cabin once the snow stops falling. Until then, visibility is so bad, we're going to get stuck again if we try to press on. And the next time, we may not get back out." He fixed her with a serious look. "It's our best option."

The idea of being stuck anywhere with Grey didn't appeal to her at all. But being stuck with him in a cabin sounded a whole lot better than the cab of the pickup truck. She grabbed her small bag and slung it over one shoulder. "Let's see if anyone's home."

CHAPTER THREE

Grey thought he'd been prepared to come face to face with Cora again. But playing through the scenario in his mind and actually seeing her was an entirely different thing.

She looked about the same as she had before. Her long, blond hair flowed over her shoulders to cascade to the middle of her back. He used to love running his fingers through her silky hair. She complained that it was too thin—too boring. He was happy to see she hadn't changed it because, as far as Grey was concerned, that couldn't be further from the truth.

It'd always been beautiful. *She'd* always been beautiful. He'd thought so since the first day he saw her in junior high. It'd only taken him a couple of years to work up the courage to ask her out, their freshman year of high school.

The first time she looked at him with love in her pretty hazel eyes, he'd been wrapped around her little finger.

Grey shook away his thoughts before he started to dwell on what had changed all of that. Instead, he watched her get out of the truck.

She may look much the same as she had five years ago,

but there was something very different about her. It was the way she carried herself. Her shoulders were back and her chin high. Not in a snobbish way, more like an air of confidence.

A general lack of faith in herself was something she'd struggled with back then. Of course, with the kind of childhood she had, it was no surprise. She'd done well for herself, considering.

Maybe that need to protect her had been part of what drew him to her in the first place. It hadn't taken long to fall hopelessly in love with her after that.

It was all in the past, though. He'd let go of his feelings for her when they divorced. They'd both moved on, and that's the way it was supposed to be. He'd thought he'd done just that, too. Until now. Some of those old feelings tried to bubble their way back to the surface. He put a lid on them and shoved them back into the closet where they belonged.

Cora didn't need him to protect her anymore. Probably didn't want it. Except here they were, stuck together in the middle of a blizzard. Those instincts to watch out for her were already kicking in again.

Snowflakes blew past her with another wind gust as they picked through the snow to the front door of the cabin. It almost gave her an ethereal quality: An image he doubted he'd forget anytime soon.

He forced his attention to the cabin. He was certain it was empty, but the last thing he wanted to do was surprise anyone. He knocked several times. When no one answered, he knocked again and accompanied that with a loud, "Hello!" Nothing.

He wasn't normally a fan of breaking and entering, but this was a different situation. "Stay here. I'll be right back." He didn't wait long enough to see if Cora would object. Instead, he jogged as best he could through the snow to the back door with a glass window in it. As was the case at every cabin, there was a covered storage shed nearby stocked with firewood. He found a piece and easily broke one panel out of the window.

Once he'd cleared away the glass debris, he reached an arm through and unlocked the door before letting himself inside.

After knocking as much snow off his boots as he could on the mat just inside, he went through the house and opened the front door for Cora. She stared at him in surprise.

"Do I want to know how you got in?"

"Probably not."

"I didn't think so." She raised her brows at him before clomping inside. She took her boots off by the door. "I'm not sure it's much warmer in here."

"I doubt it is, either." He tried the light switch nearby with no success. "They must keep the power off to the cabins that aren't rented. That or the electricity went out in the area."

Grey took his cell phone out of his pocket and tried to call his mom. Service was so poor that the call didn't go through. It could be an indication of the electricity being out for the cell tower, or maybe the storm itself was just messing with the service.

Cora watched over his shoulder. She pulled her own cell phone out but slipped it back into her pocket moments later.

"I'm going to try sending a text to my mom to let her know we're okay." Grey typed out a short note and hit send. "Sometimes texts will go through when a call can't. It's worth a try, anyway."

"I'm thankful they all got here yesterday and no one else is stuck in this."

"Me, too." Even if the power had gone out, at least his family was safe. Although the thought of them stuck in a cabin together with no way to escape sounded like a nightmare waiting to happen.

Cora craned her neck to look through the window in the front door toward the pickup truck. "I'm going to head back out and get my luggage before it gets any worse."

Grey surveyed the front living area until his gaze rested on the hearth. Everything they needed to make a fire had already been brought in and readied for the next guest. Just thinking about sitting around a warm hearth started a flood of memories. There was a time when a roaring fire was something he equated with Cora for many different reasons. But their relationship had gone cold, just like every fire eventually did. "You've already got your boots off. I'll go get your suitcase. Do you remember how to start a fire?" The encroaching memories and the emotions behind them made his question come out much more gruffly than he'd intended.

Cora frowned at him. "I can get my own bag." She spun on her heel toward the door, but Grey caught her by the elbow.

"Seriously, Cora. There's no need for you to get your boots on again when I can easily carry both suitcases back in one trip. If you don't remember how to build a fire, I'll get one going when I get back." He'd tried to soften his voice but wasn't sure how well he'd succeeded. He wasn't trying to be bossy, it was just common sense for her to stay indoors when he was still dressed for the storm outside.

She jerked her arm out of his hand. "I think I can manage." Without looking at him, she walked toward the hearth.

There were a lot of things the years might have changed about both of them, but the meaning of her walk wasn't one of them. He'd seen her mad plenty of times, especially during the last six months of their marriage. And here it'd taken him less than an hour to make her mad. Grey wasn't sure if the realization made him sadder or annoyed with himself.

He turned his frustration into action as he followed their footsteps through the snow to the truck. Flakes still fell hard as he got his carry-on bag and both of their suitcases. He locked the door of the pickup before heading back to the cabin.

Even with the heavy snowfall, it was clear the sun was getting lower in the sky. Staying at this cabin overnight was the right decision, even if the emotional air in the room might be as frigid as the temperatures outside.

He got the luggage in, closed the door behind him, and removed his boots. He wasn't ready to take off his jacket yet, though. Not until there was a fire burning in the hearth and at least some of this chill was beginning to evaporate.

"How's it going over here?" Grey crouched down beside her.

She'd gathered a lot of smaller kindling and put that in a pile. Larger pieces of kindling were in another, and finally she'd chosen a couple of logs. She turned her head to look at him. "I could get this fire started eventually, but you'll get it going faster. I don't know about you, but I'm freezing." She handed him the fire starter that had been hanging near the hearth.

He accepted her peace offering. Besides, Cora was right. He'd taught her how to make a fire a long time ago, but unless she'd become a bushcrafter since then, he still had a lot more experience.

Grey took the knife he'd used to cut down branches and went to work shaving feathers of wood off a stick into a small pile. That would ignite first and hopefully give him the time he needed to get the rest of it lit.

Ten minutes later, he was carefully breathing life into the

flame that flickered in the hearth. Only then did he realize how much the room had darkened.

When he thought it was hot enough, he added one of the larger logs. "There we go." He nodded toward the back of the cabin. "There's plenty of wood in the storage building outside. As long as we can keep this fire going, we'll at least stay warm in here."

Cora nodded. "That's good." She scooted a little closer and held her hands out toward the flame.

Grey wasn't sure if the sigh that escaped her lips was one of contentment or relief. Most likely, it was a mixture of the two.

Once that larger log caught, he added the second one and was able to sit back for a while. Suddenly, he remembered the window in the back door that he'd broken through. The chilly air would come in quickly if he didn't do something to block it. He stood again, and Cora joined him with a curious look.

He took his flashlight out, turned it on, and went down the hall to discover that the cabin had two bedrooms. He took a pillow from one of them.

Cora followed him and watched as he stuffed the pillow into the open panel of the window. Without a word, she opened several nearby cabinets and closets until she returned with a dust pan and broom. When she was done, she deposited the broken glass in the trash can underneath the sink.

They stood looking at each other, the only light coming from Grey's flashlight and what little was left from the muted daylight outside.

Grey motioned toward the cabinets. "I don't suppose you saw any food in there."

"Not a can."

He hadn't expected there to be, but something to eat sounded pretty good right now.

His phone trilled, making poor Cora jump. Grey pulled it out of his pocket, relieved to see the text. "Mom got my message. She's glad we're somewhere safe for the night. They still have power there somehow. I'm going to let her know we got a fire started."

They walked back to the living room where the fire had already begun to warm the cabin air. He noticed Cora finally unzipped her coat and hung it up on the coat rack by the front door. As soon as Grey sent his text, he did the same. He used the fire poker to adjust the wood and added another log. "It's already making a big difference in here."

"Yeah, it is." She nodded toward his phone. "Is everyone safe and warm there?"

"Yep, they're all good. Mom said they've been praying we'd find somewhere to hunker down. Flynn thinks we should try and get to the main cabin by foot tomorrow once the blizzard lets up."

Cora's eyes widened. "Do you think we could make it?"

"Definitely. It can't be more than an hour or so. Even if it's two hours, the only thing this house is offering us right now is shelter. Apparently, when Grandpa had set up reservations, he'd had the main cabin stocked with food."

As if on cue, Cora's stomach let loose with a low growl. The fire already cast an orange glow on her face, but he was certain a pink tinge had joined it.

Grey smiled at her. "You know, we're going to need some water, too." He went in search of a pan and glasses in the kitchen. He set two glasses down on a small table in the living room before stepping out on the front porch and filling the pan with snow. Once he'd returned, he put the pan near the fire so the snow would melt.

He found Cora rummaging around in her suitcase. She finally raised her hand in triumph. "Here they are." When she turned, she had a bright smile on her face. She handed him a large Ziploc bag.

Mint chocolate breakfast bars with caffeine. He couldn't stop the deep chuckle. "You brought some with you?"

She gave him a fake pout—one that had him instantly remembering what it was like to kiss those soft, warm lips of hers.

"Chocolate, caffeine, and mint. What's not to like? I knew there was no way they'd have some here."

She was right about that. Grey wasn't a fan of the protein bars, but he thought they sounded pretty good right about now. When he took a bar out for himself and another for her, Cora grinned.

"Admit it," she said as she opened hers. "You're really glad I brought these."

"I still don't understand your obsession with these, but yes, I'm glad you brought them along." She flashed him a triumphant smile. He opened his bar and took a bite. "Although, if I had my gun, I'd go out and shoot us a rabbit. Then we could have ourselves a real meal."

She rolled her eyes good naturedly. He couldn't help but relax into the comfortable rhythm of the way things used to be between them. Before she stopped opening up to him, and he started traveling more in response. Before it all fell apart.

He missed this. He missed *her* and hadn't even realized how much until now.

CHAPTER FOUR

C ora finished her protein bar and decided then and there that she'd never leave her house without one again. She knew Grey had never really liked them, but he polished his off minutes before she did. She offered him a second one, but he politely declined. He was always the planner, and she had no doubt he figured they'd better save them for tomorrow in case they weren't able to make it to the main cabin like they hoped.

She thought about Grey's family. It was going to be weird enough going to this event when she was the only outsider, but it would be even stranger to show up with Grey. Not knowing how she was going to be received by Flynn, in particular, was probably the hardest part.

Right now, however, she chose to focus on the warm cabin and the food that would be waiting there for them. Maria always had been a good cook. Truthfully, Cora had missed her as much as she had Grandpa Jackson after the divorce.

Maria had welcomed Cora from the very beginning, back when she and Grey were only partners in science class and they'd meet to put their projects together. The idea that Grey's mom looked forward to him getting home from school and even welcomed him with a snack baffled Cora. When she'd get home from school, her mom would put her to work and if she didn't get that done by dinner, then dinner didn't happen. There were days Cora ate crackers right before bed and had to struggle to get her homework done in the early hours of the morning before school began again.

Then there was Maria. Some of Cora's snacks at the Jackson home were better than the dinners she had at her own house. Once she and Grey were dating, Cora frequently ate dinner at his house. Maria never seemed to mind, and her parents never once complained that she wasn't home enough. Provided, of course, that she got her work done before she left. The homework was up to Cora. But she and Grey did theirs together, and it worked.

They worked.

Until they didn't.

Cora frowned. She instinctively pressed a hand to her lower abdomen. The large scar there always represented the breaking point in their marriage, even if things had been going downhill for a while before then.

It seemed like a lifetime ago that she'd seen the double lines on a pregnancy test. That baby was supposed to revitalize their marriage and make them realize just how much they had together. But even that plan had fallen apart.

Grey brought her back to the present when he gently nudged her arm. "You okay over there?"

She shrugged, relieved to have a distraction from the way her thoughts had been spiraling. "A little nervous about tomorrow, I guess."

"Hiking through the snow? Or seeing my family?"

Cora raised her gaze to his. "Both."

He nodded. "Well, as long as the blizzard dies down and we don't end up with twenty feet of snow out there, I'm confident we can make it to the main cabin."

His incredible sense of direction was almost maddening. Where she had to use a GPS to navigate her way to a new location multiple times before she remembered the route on her own, Grey could figure it out in his head. Worst case scenario, he used a map once and never had to use it again.

There was a time she'd affectionately referred to him as her human GPS system.

No, Cora didn't doubt that he'd get them to the main cabin tomorrow. The scarier thought was being stuck there for an extended stay when she wasn't really welcome.

Okay, so that was an exaggeration. Maria had personally encouraged her to come, not just because Grandpa Jackson wanted her to, but because Maria did as well. She'd always gotten along fine with Dare. It was Grey's older brother that she was worried about.

"Does Flynn still hate me?"

Grey was about to take a drink of water when he set the glass back down again. "He never hated you."

Cora pinned him with a serious look. As welcoming as Maria and Grandpa Jackson had been, Flynn was the opposite. He tolerated her presence and said nothing until it was clear her relationship with Grey was becoming serious. The little comments about her old clothing or how she seemed to come over just for the food hadn't gone unnoticed.

Cora could never forget the way Flynn had cornered her after she and Grey had become engaged. He told her that she needed to think long and hard about marrying into the family and then warned her against doing anything to hurt Grey.

"Really? Flynn and I have never gotten along. And he made it no secret that he blamed me for our divorce." She knew Flynn had spoken to Grey about getting a lawyer and fighting for the money and belongings. But Grey, ever the gentleman, had agreed to split it all fifty-fifty.

The resigned expression on his face told her enough. "Hate's a strong word."

"And an applicable one. I have no doubt he was celebrating the day I was no longer part of the family." Cora crossed her arms as the familiar rivers of annoyance coursed through her veins. "I can't imagine he's happy about my being here this weekend."

"No, he's not. But we've spoken about it, and he can deal. Besides, he's married, and he and Abby have two kids now, so he has something else to focus on, too." He picked up the poker and absently shifted one of the logs. "And you're right, despite my reassurances that our divorce was a mutual decision, Flynn has always put you in the blame seat. But Mom and Dare are happy that you're here, so just try not to go in swinging, okay?"

A thought came to Cora and dread slammed itself into her chest. She sat up straight, turned to face Grey, and clenched her fists. "Please tell me you never told them about—"

"No, I didn't." He let the poker clang to the bricks of the hearth and stood. "I made a promise, and I've kept it. But not telling our families about the baby was a huge mistake, Cora, and you know it."

They were going to wait and tell everyone about the pregnancy at Christmas. But less than a month before, Cora woke up to intense pain and bleeding. Thankfully, Grey hadn't been on one of his business trips. He'd raced her to the hospital where they'd discovered it was an ectopic pregnancy and her right fallopian tube had ruptured. Cora was taken into surgery where the tube was eventually removed. The last thing Cora remembered before being wheeled away was begging Grey not to tell his family.

"It wasn't a mistake. It just plain wasn't any of their business." They'd argued round and round about it for weeks and months after the surgery, but in the end, he'd honored her request to keep it all between them. Instead, he'd simply told his family that she wasn't feeling well while she recovered. "I didn't need the judgment from my parents. And the last thing I wanted was pity from your mom and judgment from Flynn."

"I get that, Cora. But what about me? I lost a baby, too." He released a heavy sigh and stood. "I'm going to go bring in some more firewood before it gets much later." He shoved his arms into his coat and then pulled his hat and gloves back on. His footsteps retreated through the kitchen before the back door opened and closed with a bang.

Cora sat in stunned silence. Of course he'd suffered a loss. But he'd taken it all in stride. She'd just assumed he'd been doing okay, that it was only her who had a hard time moving forward.

She'd spent years trying to let go of the past. If it weren't for the literal scar that had yet to fade, she might've convinced herself it'd all been a bad dream. That old phrase about time healing old wounds? Yeah, she wasn't so sure about that.

GREY WISHED the firewood hadn't already been chopped. He could use some good physical exertion right about now. He found several logs that would work well and hopefully keep the fire burning all night long. If it weren't so cold outside, he probably would've delayed his return to the house for a while. As it was, the frigid air was already seeping in after only fifteen minutes. He stacked what he could in his arms and went back inside.

He'd never understood why Cora didn't want to tell people about the baby. It bothered him to no end. Not only because he would've liked some support after finding out that the pregnancy was ectopic, but because that was when Cora really retreated from him. From their marriage.

Things weren't great before, but the loss was like a wall that neither of them could quite climb. It only got worse from there.

Watching Cora go through the grief and pain had been unbearable, and when she refused to open up to him, it was even worse. She kept trying to push him away, and eventually he let her. They'd both made a lot of mistakes.

He re-entered the living room, dropped the logs into the wood bin near the hearth, but didn't see her near the fire. "Cora?"

"On the couch."

He could barely make out her form in the ambient light from the fireplace. His heart twisted painfully in his chest. The last thing he wanted to do this weekend was fight with her. "Are you getting sleepy?"

"A little." She shifted, and a small light came on around her wrist as she checked her watch. "Wow, it's not even ten yet. How lame is that?"

"Not so lame considering all we've been through today." He turned his flashlight on. "I think it best if we sleep in here near the fire. You can have the couch, and I'll make a pallet on the floor. Does that work?"

"Yeah, that's a good idea."

On that note, he retrieved the pillows and comforters from both bedrooms. There was an extra blanket in one of the closets as well that he snagged on his way back to the living room.

Together, they moved the couch closer to the fireplace. While Cora got her spot set up, Grey folded the comforter several times to make a thick pad on the floor near the fire. Between that warmth and the blanket he found, he had no doubt he'd be comfortable enough to sleep. If anything, frequent checks on the fire to make sure it was still burning would be what kept him awake tonight.

He emptied his pockets so that sleeping in his clothes would be more comfortable, then lowered himself to the pallet. He'd certainly slept in less ideal places in the past when he used to go camping regularly. The sounds of Cora shifting on the couch quieted. While he was on the ground, he was easily within arm's reach of her.

Instead of falling asleep, Grey couldn't take his eyes off the fire. The flames danced and twisted as the wood crackled. Occasionally, a little popping noise or a slight shift in the log would cause sparks to release into the air before disappearing again.

He thought Cora was asleep when her soft voice broke the near silence. "Grey?"

"Yeah?" She was silent long enough that he started wondering if he'd imagined her speaking at all.

"I'm sorry."

Of all the things she might have said, those words surprised him the most. "For what?"

"For not realizing you weren't okay after…" Her voice broke. "You never said anything, so I guess I just figured…"

"That I didn't care?" That she could possibly think that bothered him on so many levels. It couldn't be further from the truth. "I tried to talk to you, Cora. No matter what I did, you pushed me away."

"No, you ran away." There was an edge to her voice. "When you weren't working at your family's store, you were out on a trip to find things to stock it with. We hardly saw each other."

He clenched his jaw and blew out a frustrated puff of air. "You're right. Even when we were in the same house, we rarely saw eye to eye anymore. We had medical bills that we needed to pay. At some point, traveling more just made sense."

"Don't blame me for your decision to not come home for weeks on end. That's not fair." The couch creaked, and he could see her sitting up in the fire light. "It was not all my fault."

"You're right about that. There's plenty of fault to go around."

His words seemed to diffuse the situation a little. He kept his gaze on the fire while her angry breathing calmed over time.

When she spoke again, it was so softly he barely heard her. "It seemed like you'd recovered from losing the baby. Like you'd just moved on. And I...I couldn't."

The brokenness in her voice just about did him in. He'd never been able to stand to see her hurting. "I was trying to hold it all together. For us both." He paused. "Losing that baby was hard on me, too, Cora. But watching them wheel you away for emergency surgery was the scariest moment in my life, because I was afraid I might lose you, too." The only time Grey had ever voiced any of this aloud was when he was praying while she was in surgery. "Afterward, you didn't want to tell anyone or talk about what happened."

"And that's exactly what you needed." There was no accusation in those words, only realization.

Grey's eyes slid shut. She'd needed him to be strong for

her, and he had. But at the same time, he'd needed someone to talk to. The pain and sorrow had built up until it was more than he could handle. Especially when he'd come home to find Cora clearly hurting and anything he tried to do only seemed to make it worse.

Was there something he could've done differently? He wished he knew. So much for hindsight being twenty-twenty.

CHAPTER FIVE

I t took a while for Cora to fall asleep the night before.
Their heated conversation about what happened after they
lost the baby had her replaying conversations and fights in
her head. Most of them brought back the anger and hurt that
resulted. But Grey was right about one thing: She'd tried to
close herself off from the tidal wave of emotions. By doing
so, she'd closed herself to him as well.

Cora covered a yawn and checked to make sure all her
things were back in her bags for the third time. She didn't
want to leave anything behind. Sunlight streamed through the
windows, a welcome contrast to the weather yesterday. When
she'd awakened and looked through the pane, it was a relief
to see that it was no longer snowing.

They drank some more water and had another protein bar
for breakfast. Grey found a piece of paper and left a note
with his phone number in case someone came in and found
the broken window. He had every intention of calling the
resort once he was home again to let them know what
happened.

He checked on the fire to make sure there were no sparks.

They'd left it to burn out all morning. "I think we're probably good to go whenever you're ready."

Cora already missed the warmth. "Are you sure we couldn't take some with us in the form of a torch? Maybe melt our way to the main cabin?" She was not looking forward to the hike.

He chuckled. "I wish we could. Having one more thing to carry will only slow us down." He flashed her a little smile before turning back to his own suitcase.

They hadn't said a word about their conversation last night, but things felt a little different between them now. She had no idea where that left them, though.

When they closed the cabin door behind them and stepped into the snow, Cora was amazed at just how much of it had fallen overnight. "What is this, two feet?"

"At least." He reached for her suitcase. "Here, let me carry that for a while."

She was going to argue with him, but then she tried to take several strides through the snow and thought better about it. His long legs definitely gave him an advantage in this situation. She eyed her canvas-sided suitcase. "When I get home, I'm going to buy one of those hard-sided suitcases. Preferably one that's waterproof."

Even though Grey was holding the suitcases off the ground, there was no way they were going to get to the main cabin without them getting soaked. There was nothing they could do about that, though.

In fact, thirty minutes into their hike, Cora had tossed away all concerns about her suitcase. It was her cold jeans and the snow that had fallen into her boots that stole away her focus. When the snow was that deep, boots really didn't make that much of a difference unless she'd been wearing waders.

"Remind me to stay in Texas after this weekend." She

tried not to ask how far they'd gone. "Did you know it's supposed to be seventy degrees in Denton right now?"

Grey stalled and turned to look at her. "You live in Denton? When did you leave San Antonio?"

"About six months after we signed the papers. I guess I needed to get away, you know? From reminders. From my parents. The whole shebang."

"Yeah, I get it." He paused. "I moved to Fort Worth three years ago."

Cora's jaw dropped. "Are you serious?" Here she'd assumed he still lived in San Antonio. Depending on where he lived in Fort Worth, they could potentially be just minutes away from each other. What were the odds? "Do you not work for your mom anymore?"

"I opened my own store, Defending Yesterday. I focus on firearms, knives, survival and camping equipment."

"What a great name. It sounds like it totally fits you."

"It does." He looked happy as he spoke. "I worked at the store with my family, but just needed to get out there and do something on my own. Grandpa supported my decision, and Mom understood. But Flynn accused me of running away."

He didn't say anything specifically about their divorce, but Cora got the impression that was one of the deciding factors when it came to opening his own place. "I had no idea we were living so close to each other."

"Neither did I."

They continued walking. Cora had been nervous about getting lost on their way to the main cabin. Now that the snow had stopped falling, however, the visibility was good. And apparently being able to see some landmarks was all Grey really needed to navigate successfully.

He said he'd carry her suitcase for a while, but he never

did relinquish it. He handed over his carry-on bag for her to take at one point, though.

Cora's feet were starting to feel numb from the cold. "How long until frostbite sets in?"

Before they left, they'd both put on extra socks. They'd also found some plastic wrap in the kitchen and had put that around the socks as well to hopefully keep the dampness off their feet. An hour in, though, and it wasn't doing a lot for the cold.

Grey glanced at her boots in concern. "We should only have a half hour to go at the most. Do you need to rest?"

"I'm pretty sure if I stop moving, I'll turn into an icicle."

He nodded his agreement. "We've got a good pace going here. We just need to take our minds off the cold."

"Your feet are bothering you, too?" He hadn't said a word, so Cora had assumed he was doing okay.

"Oh, yeah. Someone's going to have to stop me from just sticking them directly into the fire when we get there." He smiled at her. "So, you know about me opening my own store. What do you do now?"

"I'm a registered nurse. I work in the emergency room at Denton Regional." She didn't think Grey would look more surprised if she'd told him she'd become an astronaut. She laughed. "What?"

"Nothing. I mean, that's amazing. I have no doubt you're a fabulous nurse. I just never imagined you getting into that kind of a profession." He paused for a moment to set the suitcases down and flex his hands several times before continuing. He lifted hers a little higher. "What have you got in here? Bricks?"

She hiked up one eyebrow. "What would a nurse be if she didn't take her medical bag everywhere she goes?"

He nodded slowly, and it was clear he approved of her

being prepared. "So, what made you decide to go back to school?"

Cora sobered. "After my surgery, everything was so overwhelming. The loss. The pain—physical and emotional. It was a lot. There was a nurse that night named Josie who took care of me. Instead of just checking my vitals and giving me medication, she talked to me. She'd had a miscarriage herself and said she knew what we were going through." All of it came back as though it'd been yesterday. The bags she was carrying were getting heavy, and she shifted the straps on her shoulders. "I didn't really talk much, but just knowing that she understood made a difference. And it made me feel like a person in there instead of just another number. I thought about that a lot, and when we got divorced, I decided I needed a purpose."

"You wanted to be that person for someone else."

Cora nodded silently. "It's not an easy job, but it was worth every minute back in school." She pretty much lived paycheck to paycheck now, having used all her savings on tuition, but she was making it on her own. After relying on her parents and later Grey, it was a big thing for her.

Grey turned his head to look at her. "I'm proud of you, Cora."

There were a lot of things he could've said, but those words sent warmth from the top of her head to the tips of her toes. There was a time when they would've talked about everything, and to know he approved of what she'd been doing with her life meant a lot. She gave him a shy smile as they continued their trek.

Ten minutes later, Grey stopped walking and nudged her with his elbow. "Check it out!" He set a suitcase down and pointed to the sky.

Ahead, smoke slowly rose from a point in the trees.

"Is that the cabin?"

"It's got to be."

They grinned at each other. They couldn't quite see the building itself, but it couldn't be too much further. If it weren't for the trees, they could probably spot it now. With renewed energy, they picked up the pace and speed walked through the snow that seemed to get thicker and heavier with each step.

Suddenly, it felt as though butterflies were bouncing around in Cora's stomach and her nerves kicked into high gear. All her reasons for nearly not coming this weekend resurfaced. "So, give me an update on your siblings. You said Flynn is married now?"

"Yes, to a woman named Abby. They have a little boy named Zac, who is four, and a girl named Emma, who is two." He reached out to steady Cora when her boot hit something in the snow, nearly tripping her. "Abby's pretty nice. I never did quite understand what she saw in Flynn." He gave a dry laugh. "The kids are great, though. It's been fun being an uncle."

Cora smiled. "That's great. I'm glad Flynn found someone."

Grey nodded and then burst out laughing. "Oh, and Dare. He's pretty much the same thrill-seeker. You won't believe what he's into now."

Cora smiled at the thought of Grey's younger brother. He'd always been the guy who was pulling the perfect prank on someone, although he rarely officially got caught. It was a running joke that his mom couldn't have expected any less with a name like Dare. "I have no idea."

"He learned how to ride horses and rope cattle. He just got a job as a ranch hand of all things. As you can imagine,

Flynn was less than happy. We've got an ongoing bet on how long he'll last."

"You're joking."

"Nope."

Cora tried to picture Dare as a ranch hand and had no luck. "Wow, I guess you just never know what time will do to people, huh?"

His gaze tangled with hers for a moment as the truth of that statement sank in for both of them.

Once they got past a line of trees, a large two-story cabin stood in dark contrast to the white around it. Smoke rose from the chimney.

Cora sighed with relief. Just a few more minutes and they'd have warmth and food. Hopefully a change of clothes, too, if all their things in the suitcases hadn't been completely soaked.

Grey cleared his throat. "Now that we're almost there, I have a question I've got to ask. Am I going to have some devoted boyfriend or fiancé of yours coming after me because we just spent the night alone in a cabin in the woods?"

He sounded serious, but there was humor in his expression. A laugh erupted from Cora. "Nope, you're probably safe." After a few moments of silence, she spoke again. "How about you? Some adoring girlfriend or wife-to-be who is going to come after me for sleeping on the couch near her man?"

"Nah. You're clear this weekend."

"Well, that's a relief."

For just a moment, their mutual teasing and her excitement for all the comforts she desperately needed made her temporarily forget about the people on the other side of the door up ahead. She took two hesitant steps toward the porch and stalled.

Grey leaned down a little. "You ready for this?" His breath felt warm against her frozen cheeks.

"Not even a little."

"You just survived a blizzard, Cora. And a night in a secluded cabin with me. On top of that, we managed to not kill each other." One corner of his mouth pulled up in a crooked smile. "I'd say you've got this."

She sent up a silent prayer that she hadn't made a mistake by coming here. She appreciated Grey's confidence, she just hoped he was right.

To say Grey was looking forward to warm air and a meal was a huge understatement. At the same time, he also knew his family was on the other side of that door. Even he had to admit he was a little nervous about what it would be like to have his siblings in the same room again.

He thought about Cora. She was stepping into a group of people she hadn't seen in years with no real idea of how she was going to be received. When he'd first told his family that he and Cora were getting a divorce, the reactions of his family had run the gambit. Mom was incredibly sad, since she'd always considered Cora to be the daughter she never had. Dare genuinely felt bad for both of them. And Flynn? He didn't hesitate to tell Grey "I told you so" and then quickly shifted all blame for the divorce firmly to Cora's shoulders.

She said she was worried about Flynn being less than friendly to her. He'd tried to downplay it, but he was a little concerned about it as well. At this point, Grey really had no idea what to expect.

He reached for the door knob of the heavy, wooden front door when it twisted against his palm and swung open.

Within moments, voices ushered them into the cabin. He set the luggage on a rug near the door, so it wouldn't get the floor or carpet wet. He'd barely turned around again before Mom was hugging him close.

"I'm so glad you made it here safely. I was worried until we got your text last night. Praise God you two found a cabin to stay in." She moved to Cora and immediately engulfed her in a big hug. "Oh, sweetheart, it's so good to see you." She put her hands on Cora's shoulders and held her at arm's length so she could look at her. "You are just as beautiful as always. You'll have to promise me we'll do more than just chat on the phone after this weekend."

Cora nodded with a smile before the women embraced again.

A pang of guilt struck Grey in the chest. Mom had always talked about how Cora was like a daughter to her. When Grey and Cora divorced, he'd seen Mom go through a grieving process. Oh, she'd tried to hide it for his sake, but it was still visible. The tears shining in Mom's eyes as she studied Cora confirmed that.

Suddenly, the words his mom said sank in. She and Cora spoke on the phone? He had no idea. How often? He'd just assumed they didn't speak to her any more than he did.

Grey shook Dare's hand before pulling him in for a hug. "Good to see you, little brother. You staying out of trouble?"

Dare grinned. "You know me better than that. Since when did I stay out of trouble?"

"Since never." Grey laughed. Moving away from San Antonio had been the right decision, but he missed seeing Dare more often.

He turned to find Flynn with a hand extended. "Glad you were able to hike in. We lost power in the middle of the night. But there are fireplaces in every bedroom and plenty of food.

We're getting by just fine." Abby walked up to stand beside him, their daughter in her arms. Little Emma had the same wavy brown hair that her momma did.

Grey smiled at them both. "It's good to see you Abby." He reached out and patted Emma on the back. "My goodness, she's gotten big."

Abby nodded. "She wants to do everything her big brother does, so it's been a challenge lately." She hugged the little girl to her. "It's worth it, though." She nuzzled Emma's cheek. "It's good to see you, too." She looked at Cora curiously.

"Oh, I'm sorry. Abby, this is Cora. Cora, this Flynn's wife, Abby." He introduced Emma and then looked around for his nephew. "Where is Zac?"

He'd barely gotten the words out before the little boy ran into the room and jumped right into Grey's arms. It was only moments, though, until he wrinkled his nose and started squirming to get back down again. "You're all wet."

Grey laughed at his nephew. "We just walked through the snow for two hours, kiddo." He held his hand to the boy's chest. "Snow is up to here out there. If it'd snowed much more, you'd have to use a snorkel if you went outside."

That had Zac laughing and probably coming up with something mischievous to do. He reminded Grey of Dare a lot at that age.

Cora offered a shy smile. "It's really nice to meet you, Abby. Your children are beautiful."

"Thank you." Abby looked at her husband. The impassive expression on Flynn's face caused her smile to falter.

Grey scanned the large main room. It was the same cabin they'd stayed in every time they came here for vacation when he was a kid. Furniture had changed, but the emotional ties had not. He looked at Dare who was standing nearby. "It doesn't feel the same without Grandpa here, does it?"

Dare shook his head sadly. "You're right, it sure doesn't." He lowered his voice. "Everything going okay?" He flicked his gaze to Cora making it clear what he was talking about.

"Better than I'd expected, I guess. Though I think I was about as nervous about this combination here as I was anything."

There was no doubt Dare knew exactly what he was talking about.

Mom cleared her throat loudly, garnering everyone's attention. "I can't begin to tell you how wonderful it is to have you all under one roof. I know this would've meant a lot to Grandpa." She paused a moment. "When the lawyer first told me about his wish for all of us to meet here, I was as surprised as the rest of you. But I think it's fitting that we celebrate what would have been his ninetieth birthday in one of his favorite places."

They all nodded solemnly.

Mom continued. "Your grandpa was a good man who was here for this family no matter what. He'd be okay with us mourning the fact that he and Mamaw are both gone now, but he'd also want us to remember the many good times we've had together. He'd want us to remember how important family is, because no matter what's going on in life, we always have each other." She scanned her family with a satisfied look on her face. "I, for one, am thankful we all got here safely."

Grey wasn't sure what Mom expected from this weekend. He just hoped that the tension in the room would stay at a minimum so she wasn't disappointed.

Mom held up her hand. "Now, before Grey and Cora catch their death from standing around in wet clothes, they should go change and warm up by the fire." She put one arm around each of them. "Did you two get anything to eat?"

"We had a protein bar this morning, but we sure could use something else about now." Grey's stomach rumbled. Cora had to be starving, too. "I've heard rumors that you guys have food here."

Mom smiled brightly. "There are enough sandwich fixings in the fridge to last for days. Although we're going to need to move everything into coolers outside soon with the electricity out."

"We can take care of that after we eat," Flynn said.

Mom patted Cora kindly on the shoulder. "Follow me upstairs, and I'll show you which room is yours."

Cora nodded, obviously relieved. She retrieved her suitcase from its spot on the rug and, with one final glance in Grey's direction, the two women disappeared.

They'd barely gone out of earshot before Flynn tilted his head in Cora's direction. "I'm sorry you're having to deal with this, Grey. It's completely inappropriate for her to be here. She shouldn't have been included in this. She's not family."

Grey knew his brother wouldn't be happy about Cora, but his bluntness was still a shock. "Grandpa invited her, Flynn."

"Just because he asked her to be here doesn't mean she should've accepted." He shook his head as though he couldn't believe she'd have the audacity to do such a thing.

Grey may not have shared all the details leading to their divorce, but he'd always taken responsibility for his part in it. No matter how many times he'd told Flynn that it was a mutual decision to separate, Flynn never seemed to accept that.

He cleared his throat. "Regardless of what happened between Cora and I, she and Grandpa were close. Since this weekend is all about honoring him, it's absolutely appropriate that she be here. I think it took a lot of courage for her to come and face the unknown when it would've been much easier for her to stay home."

Flynn looked like he objected, but Abby slid an arm through his, snagging his attention. "Can you keep an eye on Zac? I'm going to go change Emma's diaper before we eat."

"Of course," Flynn said, and kissed her on the cheek.

Abby seemed to be the only one who could bring out the calmer side of Flynn anymore. She was good for him.

Dare nudged Grey hard in the ribs. "Hey, big brother. As the two eligible bachelors, we get to share a room. Come on, let's take your stuff up there and you can change before you start stinking up the place." He wrinkled his nose.

Flynn fixed him with a serious look. "I don't think you're one to talk, considering what you smell like after working with horses and cattle all day."

Grey laughed. "He has a point."

Sharing a room with Dare would certainly be entertaining. Grey followed him, luggage in hand. Once he was inside alone, he set the suitcase down and resisted the urge to flop onto the bed until he'd changed.

Thankfully, while the outside of the suitcase had gotten wet, everything within had managed to stay dry. He changed into a fresh pair of jeans and a black long-sleeved pullover shirt. His poor feet had still gotten wet despite his best efforts to avoid it. He pulled thick socks on his cold, wrinkled feet and had a feeling it would be hours before they'd return to feeling normal again.

What he really wished he could do was take a hot shower. Instead, he settled for washing his face, applying fresh deodorant, and running a comb through his hair.

He hoped Cora's clothing had stayed dry as well. He still

couldn't believe that she'd been talking to Mom all these years. Cora seemed shocked to find out he'd moved to Fort Worth. If the women didn't talk about him, what did they visit about? Then he reprimanded himself for letting his mind dwell on Cora at all.

Alright, God. We're all here now. If we can get through the next two or three days without anyone getting into a fight or offending each other, that would be great.

He included himself and Cora in his silent prayer. Just because they'd survived being stranded in a cabin for one night didn't mean things had changed between them. The fact was, once everyone made it home, Grey probably wouldn't see her again for at least another five years.

The thought bothered him a lot more than it should have.

CHAPTER SIX

A big part of Cora wanted to hide out in her room until dinner. The moment she walked in and saw the fireplace, big king-sized bed, and luxurious bathroom, she was pretty sure she could just stay there forever. When Maria had told her it was a luxurious cabin, she wasn't kidding. It was certainly a lot nicer than her apartment back home. It was a shame the electricity was out. Cora would've loved to take a hot bath and soak in the large garden tub.

Instead, she stared at her reflection in the dim bathroom mirror, lit only by the daylight coming through the small window. Her hair was a mess. Good grief. Thank goodness she'd still had her winter hat on downstairs or everyone might have thrown her back out in the snow for scaring the kids. She found her brush and some hair spray and did her best to make it presentable again. Not for the first time, she was thankful her hair was easier to manage than Jen's. She pictured her friend's frizzy hair and could only imagine how bad it would be after an adventure like the one Cora had.

The thought had her chuckling. It felt good to laugh.

She'd changed into a loose, pastel blue sweater to go

with some dry jeans. Her wet clothes hung over the shower rod in the bathroom and her shoes sat in the bathtub. It would probably take a day or two for them to dry out completely.

The need for warmth from the fireplace downstairs and some food finally drove her out of her room. She stepped into the hall with socks on her feet. Once she closed her door, Cora turned and ran right into Grey. A hand against his chest was the only thing that kept her from stumbling.

His hand immediately covered her own. "Hey."

"Hey." She cleared her throat and stepped away from him. Even as her hand fell to her side, she could still feel the warmth of his chest on her palm.

He pointed toward her room. "Looks like we're neighbors."

"Who was in charge of room assignments?"

"I think Dare may have chosen ours."

"It's probably a coincidence then. I never pictured your mom as the type to set people up. Especially when the combination had already proven unsuccessful."

Something flashed in Grey's eyes, but he covered it before she could fully understand what it meant. "Yeah, well, I haven't shared a room with Dare since we were in middle school."

Cora laughed. "That should make for an interesting couple of days for you."

"No doubt." He hesitated. "I didn't realize you still talked to Mom. I'm surprised she didn't say anything."

Cora shrugged. "That first year after we... Well, your mom called me on my birthday. So, I called her on Mother's Day like I normally would. I guess we just kept on with the traditions." She slipped her hands into the back pockets of her jeans. "She never once gave me an update on you. And from your surprise, I gather she never told you anything about me, either."

Grey shook his head. "Not a word." He looked like he wanted to say more.

She glanced at the hallway behind them and lowered her voice. "I really hope my being here doesn't mess anything up for her. I know she's excited to have everyone together under the same roof. The last thing I want is to ruin that for her."

"Even after we separated, and Flynn would blame you for everything, Mom would always put him in his place. You're the daughter she never had, Cora. I don't think she'd feel the family was complete if you weren't here."

His words brought tears to Cora's eyes. It meant the world to her that Maria had continued to keep in touch with her through the years. She nodded but didn't trust her voice to respond.

For several moments, neither of them said a word. There was a time when Cora could've watched Grey like this and known what he was thinking. But things had changed. He'd changed.

Grey cleared his throat and motioned toward the stairs. "Shall we?"

She gave a nod and led the way, trying her best to ignore the fact that he was right behind her as they descended. Her attention went to a nearby window where fluffy snowflakes fell from the sky to complete the perfect winter scene. At least it was a gentle snow and nothing like the blizzard from yesterday. It did not, however, inspire Cora to go out in the cold again. In fact, they'd be lucky to get her out of the cabin when it came time to drive to the airport.

Cora stopped at the bottom of the stairs and watched Zac and Dare wrestle on the rug. Little Emma toddled over and interrupted the match by diving on top of her big brother.

Grey chuckled. "That girl's going to be tough when she gets older."

Cora watched them with fascination and a little envy. As an only child who grew up isolated and alone most of the time, she'd often longed for a sibling to play with. Even to fight with.

They'd barely made it across the living room when Maria snagged each of their arms and pulled them in the direction of the kitchen. "When Grandpa had reserved this cabin, he also paid for the fridge to be stocked. Now, the resort was going to cater dinner last night but couldn't get here because of the storm. There's plenty of sandwich stuff and snacks to last us for several days, though." She motioned to the large island in the middle of the rustic kitchen. "Help yourselves. Once you have your plates made, you should go sit by the fire and warm up."

Apparently, once sandwich fixings were brought out, other people felt the need for something to eat. Flynn and Dare were both busy piling meats and cheeses on sandwich buns. It was interesting to see the three brothers in one room together. Flynn and Grey were both tall but favored their mother with their lighter hair and green eyes. Even though it was clear they were brothers, all similarities in personality ended there.

On the other hand, Dare must look more like their father with dark hair and brown eyes and more average in height.

Cora had spent years watching their family dynamics. Flynn was very much the protective, and sometimes bossy, older brother while Grey and Dare had always been close.

Flynn picked up two plates full of food. "I'm going to take these out and eat with Abby while the kids play. Zac ate earlier, although he'll probably still pick food off my plate." He spoke to Dare and Grey, never once meeting Cora's eyes.

"The boy never stops eating." With a half wave, he left the kitchen.

Cora chose to focus on her own plate and crafting a meal that was sure to keep her stomach happy for a while.

"Still a fan of sandwiches, I see."

She glanced over her shoulder at the sound of Grey's voice. "A good sandwich like this? Absolutely."

Dare chuckled from the other side of the island. "Is there such a thing as a bad sandwich?"

"Yes." She held hers up to show it off. "But this isn't one of them."

Dare gave her a nod of approval. "I can't argue with you there."

Cora smiled, but she meant what she said. There were years growing up when she had literally nothing but peanut butter sandwiches. It's what her parents sent her to school with. It's typically all she was fed for dinner, too. In fact, if she got jelly on her sandwich, it was a luxury.

To this day, Cora couldn't stand the flavor of peanut butter no matter what it was combined with.

When she was a child, she'd assumed that was all her parents could afford. Much later, she discovered that it was simply what her parents fed her to save money, because they ate much differently themselves.

There were many foods she'd never had until she'd started eating meals with Grey's family.

She pushed her depressing thoughts aside as she added some chips to her plate and went to sit on the hearth with her back to the flames. The warmth seeped through her sweater, and she sighed with contentment.

Soon, Grey and Dare joined her. The brothers talked about some of their favorite winter memories growing up. They laughed about the year Dare had licked a frozen metal post just to prove his tongue really would stick to it. And the time they'd gotten the rare two inches of snow in San Antonio. Flynn had spent an hour trying to make a little snowman only to have Grey run into it with his bicycle when it slid on a patch of ice.

Grey cringed. "I really did feel bad about that."

"You should have, because I had to hear about it all day from Flynn," Maria said as she approached them with Emma in her arms. She patted her salt and pepper hair with her free hand. "It's a wonder you three boys haven't stripped every bit of color from my hair years ago."

Dare stood and went to place a kiss on her cheek. "And you'd look just as beautiful, Mom."

She smacked him lightly on the shoulder, but a pleased expression lit up her face. "You go finish that sandwich."

Cora drank it all in. She'd forgotten how much she missed this family interaction. As she thought about all the things she must have missed in their lives, her contentment gave way to sadness.

When she and Grey ended their marriage, Cora lost more than a husband and her best friend, she'd lost all the people she considered family as well.

GREY LAUGHED hard as he and Dare remembered one of the pranks he'd pulled in school. He was relieved to see that Cora seemed comfortable.

Conversation switched to summer vacations as they reminisced about warmer weather. Dare held up a finger. "Do you remember that one time when we all went camping when we were little, and we'd take turns in the hammock?" She crossed her arms in front of her. "We'd pull the hammock closed and then see if we could stay in while the others tried to swing the hammock hard enough to knock us out."

Mom shook her head. "You boys were always finding ways to hurt each other. It's a wonder you all made it through childhood without more broken bones."

Grey finished his sandwich and glanced at Cora. She was laughing with the rest of them, but there was an echo of sadness in her eyes. He was surprised when his first instinct was to reach for her hand. He seriously doubted she'd welcome the sentiment.

He wondered if all their talk about childhood memories was what was making her so sad. He and Cora had spent a lot of time talking about Cora's childhood. Technically, her parents had kept her fed and clothed, and Cora had a room of her own with a few things in it. But it wasn't enough. She'd missed out on so much.

Her parents were emotionally withdrawn. They shared nothing of their love or lives with Cora. She might as well have grown up alone, and Grey had often wished he'd met her before junior high.

His family—with the exception of Flynn—had welcomed her with open arms, and she'd jumped right into them back then. Who did she have in her life now? Was she as alone now as she was before they'd met? Or had she replaced him and his family?

Mom changed the subject by asking Cora more about her job. "That sounds wonderful, Cora. I'm sure that isn't an easy job. Do you put IVs in and everything?"

Cora's eyes brightened as she spoke about a job she was clearly passionate about. "I do anything to help my patients, from drawing blood to putting in IVs. I see my job as being that bridge between them and the doctor and making them feel more comfortable during a scary or uncertain time in their lives. I know what a difference that can make."

When they were in high school, Cora had struggled with what she wanted to do with the rest of her life. Once they got married, she seemed content with a part-time job at one of the local office supply stores. He'd never expected her to take an interest in the medical field, but it clearly agreed with her.

Cora had finished her meal. She and Mom decided to go to the kitchen and organize food into coolers to set outside in the snow.

Grey watched as she left the room and could see her in the kitchen as they talked. He didn't realize he was still looking at the door she'd exited through until Dare reached over and kicked him in the shin.

Grey winced. "What was that for?"

"I figured you might like to know you're staring at your ex-wife." He raised and lowered his eyebrows several times for effect. "Something you want to share with the group?"

"Nope." Anyone else would hear Grey's tone of voice and know the topic was no longer open for discussion. Anyone but Dare, that is.

Dare glanced over to Flynn and Abby as they played with Zac. "Flynn clearly isn't happy she's here."

"Yeah, well he's not happy about a lot of things." Maybe that was rude, but it didn't make it untrue. "The way I figure it, this is a weekend to honor Grandpa. If he wanted Cora here, that should be enough."

"Agreed." Dare kicked him in the leg again. "Way to build a bridge and get over it all, bro."

"I'm serious, Dare. If you don't stop kicking me, I'm going to knock you right out the front door and into a snowbank."

"Mmm-hmm." Dare gave him a look that lived up to his

59

name. A moment or two later, he tipped his head toward the kitchen. "Seriously, though. What's it like seeing her again?"

That wasn't an easy question to answer. "It feels like it's been a dozen years, and yet just yesterday at the same time." Grey changed the subject to horses and roping, which took his little brother's attention away from Cora.

At one point, Grey noticed Mom come out and ask Flynn something before he followed her back into the kitchen. Moments later, Grey looked up again to see Flynn and Cora talking. Immediately on alert, he stayed seated, uncertain what kind of conversation they were having. He'd hoped Flynn would keep his negative comments to himself. Based on his body language, and the way Cora's expression went from neutral to pained, it was clear it was too much to ask of Flynn.

Grey interrupted Dare. "Hey, I'm going to go make sure everything's okay in there."

Dare's gaze went to the kitchen and he sobered. "When it comes to Flynn, there's a fine line between concerned big brother and bully."

"I couldn't agree with you more. I'll see you later."

Dare nodded.

As Grey got up from his seat and strode toward the kitchen, his brain told him he ought to let Cora be. She was more than tough enough to handle anything thrown at her. She'd proven that many times over the years he'd known her.

This intense need to protect her was unnecessary, but he wasn't about to ignore it either. Someone needed to show Flynn that Cora was welcome here, too.

CHAPTER SEVEN

"It wasn't easy for Grey to get his life straightened out once you walked away." Maria had gone to retrieve another box from the storage closet upstairs, and Flynn was taking advantage of the time alone with Cora.

"Grandpa Jackson wanted me here. He was like a grandfather to me, and there's no way I was going to ignore those last wishes." Cora knew Flynn had issues with her, but was it so wrong to think he could at least bury them for the weekend? If for no other reason, for Maria's sake.

Flynn frowned. "I get that, and your motivation is admirable. But if this is your way of trying to get a foot through the family door, then you are sadly mistaken. Grey moved on, and I hope you have, too."

"Of course I've moved on. I'm a registered nurse now. I have friends and a life of my own."

"And the education that made it possible for you to be a registered nurse was paid for by my brother's money."

Cora dug a fingernail into her thumb to try and curb her temper. "Grey and I are being considerate toward one another in honor of Grandpa Jackson. He doesn't have a problem with my being here, so neither should you."

A muscle in Flynn's neck flexed as he clenched his jaw. "I know you wanted to honor Grandpa Jackson's wishes, but coming here was selfish, Cora. You didn't consider how your presence would disrupt the entire family."

Maria returned then with the last box they'd need. Flynn took it from her and started filling it with food.

Flynn's words left Cora feeling numb. No matter what he said, Cora hadn't made a mistake. Coming here for Grandpa Jackson was the right thing to do.

But it did leave her wondering whether she was doing more harm than good. She loved Maria, and despite all they'd gone through, she'd always love Grey. Was Cora only making it harder on them both? Hurting them was the last thing she wanted to do.

There wasn't a thing she could change now, though. It's not like she could just hike to the airport and get on the first flight home.

An overwhelming sadness enveloped her as she decided to go back to her room for a while. She'd gotten halfway up the stairs when Grey called to her.

"Cora, wait up a second."

She swallowed hard and did her best to paste a normal smile on her face. "Hey. What's up?"

"Are you okay?"

"Sure." That was a lie, and it was clear he knew it, too. "I'm just going to go up to my room for the afternoon."

Grey put a hand on the rail next to Cora. "I only heard the last part of the conversation, but Flynn—"

Cora shook her head to stop him. "I handled it. I came here to honor Grandpa Jackson. I can survive anything for two or three days, right?" She gave him a sad smile and continued her walk up the stairs. She could tell by the footsteps behind her that he was following. When they got to her door, she turned around again. "Let it go, Grey."

"I'll talk to Flynn. He needs to leave you alone, especially when it comes to us. That's our business and not his."

"There is no 'us' anymore, remember?" Her voice sounded much sadder than she wanted it to. "You can't fix everything. I'm going to go read for a while. Seriously, Grey, go visit with your family. I think it's great you're all together again. It was a long time coming."

She slipped into her room, closed the door behind her, and turned the lock. She leaned against the doorframe and noted that it was several heartbeats before Grey's footsteps faded.

One tear escaped to slip down her cheek, but that was all she'd allow. She'd cried way too many tears over Grey. Over this family. She was supposed to have moved on, and it'd do her well to remember that.

Cora spent the rest of the afternoon in her room. She had an entire library stored on the reading application on her phone. Since the electricity was out, though, she turned it off to conserve what battery power she had left.

Thankfully, she'd also tucked a paperback into her suitcase. It was one she'd purchased at the bookstore last month during an author signing. She didn't buy that many paperbacks anymore, but this weekend convinced her she should always have something to read because you just never knew when you might have some spare time.

She read for a couple of hours before falling asleep on the bed, her book propped open on her stomach. The sounds of voices outside along with a child's squeal woke her up. A glance at her watch told her it was five-thirty. She supposed she should probably clean up and meander downstairs soon.

Cora had just finished washing her face and double

checking her hair when there was a tap on the door. She opened it to find Maria waiting with a smile.

"I thought I'd check on you and see how you were doing." Maria nodded to the room behind Cora. "Do you have everything you need?"

"Most definitely." Cora lowered her voice. "Even without electricity, this place is nicer than my apartment back home. It's downright luxurious."

Maria smiled. "It is lovely, isn't it?" She rested one hand against the doorframe. "I'm glad we have memories of spending vacations here with Grandpa Jackson. I only wish you could've come here with us once. We'd have dance parties, play poker, and roast hot dogs and s'mores over the fire." Her sigh had a hint of sadness.

Cora nodded. "He was an amazing guy. I wish I could've met his wife." She knew her voice sounded wistful. She'd loved having a surrogate grandfather but had often wished she'd had a surrogate grandmother as well. She imagined baking with her or having tea parties as a child. All those fun grandmother/granddaughter things she'd read about in books but had never experienced herself.

"She would've loved you, sweetheart." Maria reached out to tweak a little of Cora's hair. "Come on, I want you to sit with me at dinner tonight. I have a feeling one of my sons hasn't been overly welcoming, and I want to make sure he knows that you have support here."

"Oh, you don't have to do that, Maria. I'll be fine up here."

"Nonsense. I guarantee you that he's alone in his opinions."

"The last thing I want to do is make it harder on you and Grey." Her voice caught.

Maria pulled her into a hug then. "Believe me when I say

that you'll always be a part of this family. You've been missed, girl. I love having you here, and I don't think Grey minds even the tiniest bit." She leaned away enough to give Cora a wink. "Don't let the thoughtless words of someone who can't let go of the past ruin this, okay?" She looked at the empty fireplace. "Besides, it's getting cold up here. I'll have Grey come and light the fire before you retire tonight." Maria offered her a sweet smile. "So, what do you say? Are you going to make me stand here all night, or are you coming downstairs with me?"

There was no sense in arguing with her. There'd never been any doubt where Grey's stubbornness had come from. Cora returned the smile. "Thank you, Maria. Let me grab something quick and I'll be ready to go." Knowing she'd have a place to sit and someone to visit with boosted her mood.

When they got downstairs, Grey caught her eyes and mouthed, "You okay?"

She gave him a subtle nod and then tried to ignore the warmth that surrounded her heart in response to his concern.

Everyone took a seat and bowed their heads as Maria began to pray.

"Father, we praise You. Not only for the opportunity to gather together, but for safely bringing us through a variety of challenging circumstances. It's too easy to focus on the things that seem to be falling apart around us. Help us to focus on You, grow closer to each other, and make the most of our time here. Please bless this food to the nourishment of our bodies. In Your Son's name we pray."

"Amen," the word was echoed all around the table.

The anxiety weighing on Cora's heart dissipated a little as she glanced around the table. In this moment, everything seemed to be okay. This right here was exactly what Grandpa Jackson had wanted.

Cora felt a strange mix of contentment and sadness. It was weird to be back with the family she loved, yet very much as an outsider.

AFTER DINNER, Abby brought some toys and a puzzle down for the kids while the adults got comfortable in the living room to discuss their situation. Even with the fading sunlight, the glow from the fire made it easy enough for them to see each other. Grey chose to sit on the couch between Dare and Cora.

"We still don't have cell service, so it's hard to know what's going on at the resort or anywhere else," Flynn was saying. "They're used to a lot of snow here. I'm assuming, now that the blizzard itself is over, they'll be dispatching snowplows to clear the roads in the next day or two."

Dare nodded. "I can't imagine that we'd be stuck here much longer than that."

"We've got plenty of food to last us," Mom told them. "Between all of the sandwich fixings that were left behind, plus breakfast stuff, we're probably good for at least three days."

Grey turned to Abby. "How are you on diapers for Emma?"

"We brought enough to hopefully get us through Monday if necessary. After that, we'll be scrambling."

"Nothing like situational potty training," Mom said with a chuckle. "I'm kidding. We can make some cloth diapers if it comes down to it." She patted Abby's arm.

It was Saturday night now. Grey hoped it wouldn't be

much longer than an extra day or two. The sun shone all day, although the temperature never did rise above freezing so the snow situation hadn't changed. If anything, they received a little more accumulation first thing in the morning.

"What about medication?" Cora's voice snagged his attention. "Is everyone good on that front?"

Everyone looked at each other around the room and no one spoke up. Cora looked satisfied with that.

"We also have more than enough firewood in the storage building out back to last us several days," Grey reported.

"So, we just sit here and wait to be rescued?" It was clear by Abby's voice that she wasn't a huge fan of that idea. "Chances are, the airport was one of the first places they plowed. Why can't we try to make it there tomorrow as planned?" She exchanged a look with Flynn.

"Because we can't see the roads." Grey motioned through the window at the darkening sky. "Here we have food, water, and shelter. If anyone tries to drive out now and gets stuck, it could be potentially dangerous. At this point, the airline will have to help switch everyone's tickets and move things around. We'll get home, it just may be a mess."

Abby glanced at Flynn who put an arm around her shoulders in response. Another look passed between them, one that had Grey wondering if there was a particular reason why they wanted to get out of here so badly. Surely a reason beyond getting away from Cora.

Mom looked around the table. "You know, I think Grandpa would get a kick out of the fact that we're all stuck here like this. He always used to say that sometimes it takes something drastic to bring people together, and I think that's what this weekend was all about." She looked around the room with tears in her eyes. "I think we need to try to get together like this more. It doesn't really matter what the occasion is, as long as we make sure we don't lose touch with each other." She put an arm around Cora, who was sitting next to her. "Too much time has already gone by. If there's one thing that Grandpa's passing should have taught us, it's that time is too precious to waste." She used her napkin to wipe at the tears that threatened to escape and laughed. "Speaking of being too precious to waste, I just may have some dessert I've been saving for tonight. Cora, would you mind giving me a hand?"

Cora smiled and followed Mom into the kitchen. They returned with a frosted chocolate cake, a plate of cookies, and napkins.

"Dessert was included with all the sandwich fixings, but I wanted to save the cake until everyone was here together. It seemed fitting to celebrate Grandpa's birthday."

Murmurs of approval followed her words. At the mere mention of cake, Zac abandoned his game and came running for his sugar fix.

Once everyone had their cake, they settled down to eat. Mom addressed Cora. "Will the hospital understand if you don't show up for work on Monday?"

Cora swallowed her bite. "My boss knows where I am, and I mentioned the storms they were expecting here. I'd like to actually contact him so he knows to get another nurse in to cover my shift, but there's nothing I can do about that." She shrugged. "But I'm not worried about losing my job or anything. Registered nurses are in high demand. With any luck, we'll get power back tomorrow so I can call in."

Dare grimaced. "I may not be so lucky. I just started working at this ranch a couple months ago, and the owner isn't the nicest guy I've ever met."

Flynn said nothing as he focused on his dessert. Grey couldn't imagine he had much to worry about with the family store. They'd had a great manager working for them for years. It was the same with Grey and his store. Brody had things under control.

Once dessert was finished, everyone dispersed. Grey found Cora looking out the living room window. It was dark outside, but between the moon in the sky and the bright white snow, they could still make out the shapes of items on the porch and the trees beyond. Grey went to stand behind her. "I don't know about you, but I'm glad we're not hiking out in that again."

She chuckled. "Yeah, me, too."

He studied her profile. "Look, when you decided to come up here for Grandpa, I know you didn't sign up for all of this. Hiking to the cabin or getting stuck. I'm sorry it's harder than it should've been."

"It's okay. Really." She paused for several moments. "Am I the only one who suddenly feels as though we've lived a lifetime in the last five years?"

Her words hit on exactly how he was feeling. He thought he wanted to keep distance between them. But now that they were here, he felt like he'd missed so much of her life. It's not like he'd expected any different, but the reality was still a bit hard to swallow.

"No. It's not just you." For the first time in a while, a pang of regret threaded its way through his memories of the last months of their marriage.

Her lashes lifted, and her pretty hazel eyes focused on him. How many times had he gotten lost in those eyes when they were together? Their effect hadn't diminished. If things had gone differently, and they'd never separated, this weekend would probably be a romantic getaway.

He wasn't sure which of them broke eye contact first. She

looked as though she were going to say something and changed her mind.

"I have a crazy idea." His words brought her gaze back to his. "What if, just for the rest of this weekend, we pretend we're friends again?"

Cora's eyes widened as she seemed to consider his suggestion —one he'd completely spoken on a whim, but now hoped she'd agree to. They'd been best friends for a long time, surely they could remember how to find a little of that now.

"Come on." He nudged her shoulder with his arm. "What do you say? Temporary truce?"

A quiet chuckle accompanied a small smile on her face. "Sure. How hard can it be, right?"

CHAPTER EIGHT

The temperature in the cabin wasn't too cold if you were in the main room with the large fireplace or the attached dining room. The rest of it, however, was quite chilly. Thank goodness each bedroom had a fireplace in it. Since he and Cora had only arrived that morning—had it just been a few hours ago?— her fireplace would need to be lit. He volunteered to accompany her and help, and she agreed.

Frosty air engulfed them the moment they opened the door to her room. Cora crossed her arms in front of her. "It may be a while before it's warm enough to go to sleep."

Grey thought about last night and how comfortable it ended up being in the little cabin. Between the warm fire, blankets, and sleeping so near the hearth, he hadn't felt the effects of the cold weather outside at all. And the company? Well, that was complicated.

The only light in the room came from Grey's flashlight. He handed it to Cora who kept the beam trained on the hearth. It wasn't long before he had a roaring fire going. The flames cut through the darkness just like the warmth began to carve a space in the night's chill.

MELANIE D. SNITKER

He got the comforter off the bed, folded it, and set it on the floor near the hearth.

"Thank you." Cora smiled at him as she sat down and scooted closer to the fire. "I remember the first time I watched you build a fire."

Grey eased himself down next to her. "Our senior year. You were so nervous about going camping for the first time."

When Grandpa Jackson heard that Cora had never been camping in her life, he knew they had to change that. Their church organized a family campout every summer, and Grey invited her to come along. He never had to worry about whether she'd do okay without the many comforts of home. The poor girl had just been excited to get away from her parents.

She'd taken everything in from how to build a fire to roasting marshmallows over it.

The memory of kissing away a bit of sticky marshmallow from the corner of her mouth flooded his mind.

With the way she was staring into the building flames with a faraway look, he wondered if she was remembering the same thing.

"It was really nice of your mom and Grandpa Jackson to include me as much as they did. I've always appreciated that." She rubbed her hands together in front of the fire, clearly enjoying the warmth that emanated from the flames.

"What's going on with your parents now?"

She shrugged. "They're still together in a very dysfunctional marriage. He's gone half the time, but I don't think she really cares. They still like to throw it in my face that I couldn't hold my marriage together while theirs is still successful. Well, their definition of successful, anyway." Cora glanced at him with a cringe. "Sorry."

He held a hand up to let her know he hadn't taken

72

offense. It didn't surprise him at all that her parents had rubbed Cora's nose in it.

"Anyway, they still live in San Antonio. I think it's been over a year since the last time I saw them, and sadly, that's okay with me."

"Putting space between you and the two of them is good." Grey had always felt they had a toxic effect on Cora. The few times he had been around her parents had left him feeling helpless and angry about the way they treated her. "In my opinion, the kind of relationship your parents have isn't healthy, regardless of whether they are married or not."

"I agree with you." Cora's hands must have warmed up enough because she let them fall to her knees. "But it does sting a little, you know?" She gave him a sideways look. "There were only a handful of things I was determined to do better than my parents, and marriage was one of them."

"Well, it wasn't just you." Now that the fire was burning steadily, Grey was able to relax more. His arm rested against hers. She didn't shift away and neither did he. He didn't want to.

For now, he wanted to steer their conversation back to a simpler time. "We did have a lot of fun back in the day."

"We sure did." Cora's voice sounded wistful. "I miss it."

"Yeah. Me, too." He paused. "I miss us. The way it used to be between us."

She let her head tilt a little to rest lightly against his upper arm. She said nothing, but her action spoke of a similar feeling of loss.

Grey had been convinced that keeping his distance after the divorce was the smart thing to do. Maybe it was—in the beginning.

Now? Sitting here with Cora felt like all kinds of right.

✳

Cora's heart pounded a warning as she leaned into Grey's arm. Seriously, this was one of the stupidest things she could be doing right now. Yet, the intense feeling of security coupled with the overwhelming sense of nostalgia meant the last thing she wanted to do was move.

She'd spent months—years—moving past all of this. She'd left Grey and their love behind. It hadn't been easy, but she'd done it.

This right here felt like a giant step backwards. A step she wasn't willing to take, no matter how temping it might be. Besides, sitting together in the dark out of necessity given the circumstance didn't exactly create the perfect get-back-together scenario. The truth of the matter was, as soon as the roads cleared, they'd both go their separate ways. To their separate lives.

Cora suppressed a groan. The warmth of his arm penetrated her temple. When he rested his cheek against the top of her head, her right hand itched to reach for his. As though, even after all these years, they knew they were supposed to connect. The need to thread her fingers through his was so insistent, it finally gave her the strength to put good sense into action. She abruptly sat up straight and then tried to make it look subtle. At least he couldn't see the pink tinging her cheeks in the firelight, right?

"You said you didn't have a girlfriend right now. Why is that?"

Grey shifted away from her and reached for the fireplace poker to move a log a little closer to the flame. He didn't look at all comfortable with this line of conversation. "I haven't done much dating the last couple of months. I broke up with someone right before Grandpa died, and then I guess it just hasn't been a priority since then."

"I can imagine." Cora had to make a conscious effort to keep her face neutral. Of course he dated. She truly wasn't surprised. It sounded like he'd probably be seeing someone now if it weren't for the trauma of Grandpa Jackson's passing.

"What about you? Why aren't you remarried?" He spoke the questions simply, but his voice sounded strange.

Cora blinked at him. He was watching her carefully now as she considered her words. "I don't know. If I couldn't make marriage work with my best friend... I guess I'm not sure I'd want to risk messing that up a second time." She hadn't meant to be quite so honest with him. "As for dating, my friend likes to regularly set me up with guys without letting me know ahead of time. I can't say I'm a fan, and I don't think she cares." She forced a small laugh. "I prefer group gatherings. Takes the pressure off."

Grey nodded. "That makes a lot of sense. It's easier to get to know someone and see who they really are that way." He studied her thoughtfully.

Was he mentally reliving the many group gatherings they'd gone to before finally dating each other? That was how Cora had discovered he was a gentleman, and that he'd defend just about anyone who was getting picked on, no matter who they were.

And that included her. She'd never really fit in at school and was often a target for bullies.

Man, Grey was her hero back then. She'd looked to him for everything from reassurance to friendship. She'd like to think she'd been there for him, too.

She wished she could go back and pinpoint where it all

went wrong with them. She suspected it was a lot of things that gradually grew into something much bigger.

"Grey?" The word was out of her mouth before she realized she was going to say it.

"Yeah?" She shook her head, but he cupped her elbow in his hand to bring her gaze to his. "What is it?"

"When we were married, it felt like we went from being happy to everything falling apart around us with very little in between." She paused. "Was it like that for you, too? Or was I just naïve? Or stupid?"

"If you were, so was I." He gave her a sad smile. "That's how I felt, too." His hand moved from her elbow, down her arm, and paused when their hands touched.

Electrical impulses sparked at every point where her fingers met his. In that moment, it'd be too easy to pretend as though they were reliving a simpler time in their lives. Too easy to allow herself to lean into him and forget the pain that had punctuated the last six months of their marriage and the years that followed.

He must have come to the same conclusion because they moved away from each other at the same moment.

"I'm going to go and let you get some rest." He tried for a normal smile and nearly succeeded. "Good night, Cora. I'll see you tomorrow."

"Good night."

He closed the door softly behind him leaving Cora alone. Instead of letting her mind wander, she busied herself changing into sweatpants and an oversized, long-sleeved shirt to sleep in. By the time she'd used the bathroom and brushed through her hair, the room was nice and warm. She crawled between the sheets of the bed and allowed her head to sink into the oversized pillow.

Had she really only flown into Colorado yesterday? It felt

like so much longer since she'd left Denton. She thought about her life and everything she'd accomplished in the last few years.

Being a nurse was a dream come true. She could help others, and she was respected. During her shifts at the hospital, Cora was truly happy to be needed and to make a difference in other people's lives. But when she went back to her apartment at the end of the day? The time dragged, and Cora often felt trapped. Technically, she had everything she needed there, but it wasn't home.

The realization hit her with a flood of emotions that she had to work to swallow back. To her, home had been Grandpa Jackson and Maria's house. Later, it'd been the home she shared with Grey.

"I'm in a good place right now, God. I know that, and I'm thankful." Cora swallowed her tears as she stared at the weird shadows that danced across the ceiling in time to the flames in the hearth. "I just sometimes wonder if I'll ever get to a point in my life when it feels like home again."

AFTER GREY LEFT Cora's room, he'd gone back downstairs to help Mom with anything he could possibly think of to do. The last thing he wanted was to replay his conversation with Cora. When he got to his room, he found Dare had beat him there and already had the fire blazing. The warmth welcomed him in, and Grey collapsed onto the small couch.

"That bad, huh?" Dare was looking at him with a mixture of curiosity and amusement. "You and Flynn haven't been in a fistfight yet, so I'd say the weekend is going better than a lot of us feared it would."

"Funny." He looked for something nearby to chuck at his

brother and finally resorted to one of his own shoes. Dare easily ducked out of the way. Grey took the other off and tossed it to the floor.

"In all seriousness, though, is Cora doing okay? All of this can't be easy."

"I think so. She didn't really want to talk about it." He gave his brother a pointed look. Maybe Dare would get the hint and realize that Grey didn't particularly want to talk about Cora right now, either.

Dare joined him on the couch. "So, what's it like?"

"What's what like?" As if he didn't know. But if Dare was going to ask a stupid question, Grey was going to make him ask a complete one.

"Spending time with Cora?"

Grey decided to go with nonchalant. "It's been fine. I found out she's living in the Fort Worth area, too. Neither of us had any idea we lived so close."

"That's pretty interesting." He was clearly waiting for more information. "So that's it? All is fine in the world of Grey and Cora? Wow, how dull."

"I'm sorry if our relationship bores you." Grey shot him a sharp look.

"Then there's still a relationship?" Dare's eyes twinkled.

It was a slip of the tongue, but that didn't matter now. Once Dare grabbed a hold of something, he rarely let it go. He was a lot like a pit bull in that respect. "No, no relationship. I should've said friendship, and even that is shaky at best." He tried to shove Dare off the couch, but his younger brother swerved out of the way and stood again.

"Are you telling me there are no sparks this weekend? No interest at all between the two of you?" Dare's voice sounded dubious. "I find that very hard to believe. I'm pretty sure

Grandpa had the two of you in mind when he concocted this whole weekend."

Grey would find this whole thing amusing if it didn't center around him and his lack of a marriage. Grandpa had been an old romantic, and Dare had certainly inherited that trait. If Dare ever met the right woman and put his mind to it, he would have no trouble wooing her. "Or maybe Grandpa was hoping to smooth things over between the two of us and Flynn."

"Well, yeah, that too." Dare gave him a confident grin. "You didn't answer my question."

"We both went our separate ways. Five years is a long time, Dare, and if you or Grandpa thought that a weekend would change that, you are seriously reaching."

Dare didn't look convinced. "Well, that works out pretty well for me."

"How do you figure?"

He put a hand to his chest then pointed to the wall between their room and Cora's. "Come on, Grey. A smart blonde who's dedicated enough to go back to school to pursue a career? She's totally my type. And now that we're both single and unattached, the timing could be right."

Grey pushed himself off the couch and stood toe-to-toe with Dare. "Don't make the mistake of thinking Flynn's the only one I could get in a fistfight with." They'd only had one, and it was back in their teen years. Their family didn't let them forget it, though.

Dare put a hand on Grey's clenched fist and pushed it down. "Easy, boy." He laughed.

Grey seriously considered punching him anyway. "I'm glad you're enjoying yourself."

"Maybe you should think about whether you object to the idea of my dating Cora because I'm your brother, or if it's because you've still got the hots for her and won't admit it." Dare whistled as he strutted to one of the beds and flopped onto his back.

He wasn't sure what annoyed him more: That Dare had baited him into responding, or that he was partially right.

Dare spoke again from the bed. "Maybe all of this is God's way of giving you two a second chance."

CHAPTER NINE

W hen Cora woke the next morning, the air in her room was cool. She turned her head to see that the fire had gone out at some point during the night. She'd had every intention of waking up and adding a log or two, but apparently sleep had been more important. She didn't think she'd moved all night.

Now that she was warm under the covers, she hesitated to break that bubble by getting up. In fact, if her book had been within reach and not back in her suitcase, she might have reached for that and not bothered to get up for breakfast.

It was already light outside. Curiosity finally got the better of her, and she reached for her watch on the wide table. It was after eight? Wow, she must've been tired. She listened intently but heard nothing from the hallway outside of her room. Either everyone else was sleeping in as well, or they were downstairs.

The lyrics to Out of Eden's song, "Lovely Day," played through her mind. "Okay, God. Yesterday was a bit of a beating. Any chance You could ease up on us a bit today?" No response, not that she'd necessarily expected one. It always seemed like she got the answers to her questions in some of the strangest ways.

She was more worried about dealing with Flynn if he kept pushing her today. The last thing she wanted to do was ruin this weekend for Maria or the others. "Please give me an extra dose of patience today. I think I'm going to need it."

The promise of pastries finally drove Cora out of bed. She wasn't about to jump into the shower with only cold water available, but she did use a washcloth as a sort of sponge bath, which was bad enough.

Once she was cleaned up and dressed, she headed downstairs while singing the lyrics from the same song to herself.

Cora expected to see almost everyone, but only Abby and Emma were sitting on the couch. "Wow, I figured I was the last one to wake up."

Abby smiled as she held Emma on her lap. "Mom just went upstairs again to change. Dare and Grey went outside to get more firewood. Poor Flynn is probably still trying to wrestle Zac into some clean clothes." She rolled her eyes good naturedly. "Our son would prefer to be a nudist if it were up to him."

Cora laughed hard at that. "I imagine keeping him clothed can be a challenge at times, then."

"Definitely." Abby had cut up a donut and was handing bite-sized pieces to Emma. "I'm really glad I finally got the chance to meet you. I've heard a lot of different things…" She paused and started over. "I'm a big fan of drawing my own conclusions."

Cora appreciated that. "It can't be easy. There's years of history and a lot of hurt feelings. Sometimes it all seems muddled to me, and I lived through it." Emma walked over to Cora and put a chubby hand on her knee. Cora smiled at her and was rewarded with one in return. "I'm glad to meet you as well. And your children. They both seem like sweethearts."

"Thank you."

The women smiled at each other, and Cora thought that, in another time and place, they might be friends.

Emma continued to smile up at Cora and finally lifted her arms as though she wanted to be picked up. Cora glanced at Abby. "Is it okay?"

"Sure. Emma's entire life is a battle between wanting to be cuddled, and the need to run at top speed. You're looking at the lull before the sugar high hits."

Cora chuckled as she lifted Emma onto her lap. The little girl leaned into her chest and popped a thumb into her mouth, effectively melting Cora's heart.

The back door opened and banged shut. The sound of deep voices preceded the men into the living room. Between the two of them, they carried enough wood to keep the fire stoked for at least the first half of the day.

Grey took his gloves off and set them on the hearth. When he turned, he regarded Cora and Emma with a mixture of curiosity and something else Cora couldn't quite identify. She offered him a small smile before turning her attention back to the little one on her lap.

She'd always liked children, she just hadn't had a lot of opportunities to interact with them in the past. Helping them in the ER was rewarding, but they were often either too scared or too sick to really relax.

This was different, and it was impossible to not think about the baby she and Grey lost. She would've spent hours holding, feeding, and consoling their child.

She took in Emma's pretty eyes and silky hair and wondered what their baby would've looked like.

Cora had to shove those thoughts away before her

emotions got the best of her. The last thing she needed to do was look sad in front of everyone else and have to come up with some alternative reason for how she was reacting.

Abby's voice brought Cora out of her own mind.

"What's that for?"

Cora looked up to find Dare still holding onto a piece of wood he'd found outside.

"I figured I may as well take advantage of all the time we'll have today and carve something." Dare sat down on the hearth.

Cora forgot until then that he used to carve things all the time when she and Grey were married. He was actually quite good. The most impressive thing she could remember was when he turned a thick piece of wood into a fish. He later hung it up on the wall and joked that it was the only one he'd caught that weekend.

Grey pointed toward the kitchen. "You'd better find something to catch the shavings or Mom will not be happy."

"You make a valid point." Dare set the piece of wood on the ground and went in search of something he could use.

Apparently, Emma got her second wind. She climbed out of Cora's lap and ran toward Flynn and Zac who were coming down the stairs. Flynn swung her into his arms and planted a kiss on her cheek.

Cora missed holding the little girl as soon as her arms were empty.

Grey was watching her again, and this time there was no missing the longing in his eyes. She knew, because she felt it, too. Unexpected tears clogged her throat and she stood to her feet. "I'm going to go see what I can find for breakfast. I'll be back in a moment."

※

WHEN GREY ENTERED the living room and found Cora holding Emma, everything about the scene had his heart twisting painfully in his chest. He'd wanted this with Cora from the very beginning: Children. A family. Watching her hold Emma was both difficult and sweet all rolled into one.

It only took a moment after she excused herself from the room for Grey to decide to follow her. The air was noticeably chillier as he walked away from the fireplace and ventured into the kitchen. She'd gotten a napkin but was just staring at the variety of pastries Mom had set out on the bar.

"It's a hard choice, isn't it?" Grey moved to stand beside her. "Grandpa always loved the food during these trips. He sure thought of everything when he reserved this place."

Cora turned her head to look at him. There was still a hint of sadness in her eyes. "Our mess aside, your mom seems thrilled about this weekend."

Grey nodded and lowered his voice. "It's been hard on her and Flynn. The family business was something Grandpa had overseen, and I think there are those reminders everywhere. For better or worse, I think they both needed to get away." He finally chose a glazed donut with what looked like cream frosting inside and took a bite. The sugary pastry nearly melted in his mouth.

She picked out a bear claw with apple cinnamon and put it on her napkin. "I wish family didn't have to be so complicated."

He moved to lean against one of the counters and was happy when she joined him. "I guess it's never easy, whether you're talking about a family of two, or the entire extended family." They'd certainly found that out first-hand.

"Grey? Did we give up too easily?"

He was in the middle of a bite and her question had him coughing through it. He looked at her to find she was completely serious, her hazel eyes vulnerable as she watched him and waited for an answer.

Grey let her question sink in and was about to say something when Dare walked in.

"Oh, good. I'm glad there are some of the apple cinnamon ones left." He snatched a bear claw and then gave Cora a nod of approval. "Good choice." He took a large bite.

Cora lifted her own in agreement. "Absolutely. Maybe we should hide the rest for tomorrow morning." She smiled at Dare and avoided looking at Grey completely.

"Now that is an excellent idea." Dare's eyes twinkled. "I guess Zac's been asking to go outside and have a snowball fight. Flynn says none of them slept well and hinted that, if I took him outside, I could get some good uncle-nephew bonding time and the rest of them could catch a nap. Subtle, right?" He didn't look like he minded at all. "I don't suppose you two would like to join me in playing the doting aunt and uncle here in a while."

A snowball fight would help break up the afternoon. "I'm game."

"Sweet! Cora?"

Grey stepped in for her. "She's never been a huge fan of snow, Dare. She'd probably rather stay inside."

She gave him a sharp look as though she didn't appreciate him answering for her. "No, it's fine. I'll come out for a little while at least." She almost sounded enthusiastic. "Everyone should participate in a snowball fight at least once in their life, right?"

Now that Grey thought about it, they never did have much snow while he and Cora were married. She'd never been in a snowball fight? This was the weekend to change that.

Mom came in then. "I'll have to turn my cell phone on

long enough to get some pictures and a video. This is going to be fun." She chuckled as she chose a donut for herself.

Cora glanced at Grey. "I think I'll go see what's going on in the living room. If I don't sit down while I eat, I'm going to drop it. Then I'll have to be forced to eat this bear claw right off the floor because it's *not* going to waste."

Grey watched her leave the room before finally turning his attention back to his donut.

"Sorry if I interrupted something when I came in." Dare looked contrite with a dash of concern thrown in. His comment had Mom's attention.

She lowered her voice. "I know this wasn't the easiest situation for either of you, but I admire you both for sticking it out and doing it with a lot more grace than you could have. Your grandpa would be proud of you."

"Thanks, Mom. It's been harder—and easier—than I thought it'd be. Seeing her again like this."

"Why easier?" Mom took a bite of her chocolate donut and nodded approvingly.

Grey pulled a bar stool over for her to sit on and Dare followed with two more so they could join her. Grey wasn't sure he wanted to talk about this. He glanced through the kitchen door to make sure no one was close enough to over-hear their conversation.

"We were good friends before we got married, but we lost a lot of that by the time the divorce came through. I guess I didn't expect some of that friendship to still be intact when I saw her again."

"So, what is making it harder?"

Grey had to think about that for several moments. "I guess it makes it harder to remember why we called it quits in the first place." There. He'd said it.

Cora had asked him if they gave up too easily. If she'd

posed the same question to him back then, he would've told her "no" without hesitation. But now? He didn't know. Which bothered him just as much, because if there was even a possibility that they'd walked away from something that could've been fixed… The thought turned his stomach. He balled his napkin, along with the last bite of his donut, and threw it in the trash. "Did you know she and I both live in the DFW area now?"

Mom nodded. "Yep."

"I didn't realize she talked to you on a regular basis." He paused, waiting for Mom to say something. When she didn't, Grey finally asked, "Why didn't you say anything?"

"For the same reason I didn't say anything to her, either. Grey, your relationship and history are between the two of you. I decided years ago to stay out of it. At the same time, I care about both of you. Enough that I never wanted to choose between you, so I didn't."

There wasn't a thing Grey could say to that. He respected her for keeping out of their relationship, and he was glad she'd stayed in contact with Cora. "Thanks, Mom."

"Are you kidding? It was as much for me as it was for her." She stood and gave Grey a hug "You'd better go warm up by the fire before you're outside freezing your tush off."

Grey chuckled. "That's probably not a half-bad idea."

CHAPTER TEN

Grey learned something new about his nephew: He was ruthless. It didn't matter that Grey was taking it easy on the little guy and making sure he didn't hit the kid in the face with a snowball, because Zac certainly wasn't worried about the opposite. And Zac had some crazy good aim for a four-year-old.

Grey ducked behind a tree and took the glove off his right hand. He used his little finger to try and dig the snow out of his ear. Laughter floated through the air, drawing his attention to Cora who had also taken refuge behind a nearby tree. "Oh, you think that's funny, do you?"

She snorted then slapped a hand over her mouth. Her eyes were wide with humor as she nodded.

He loved seeing her like this, with her nose and cheeks red from the cold and her eyes sparkling. It was as though the snow had scrubbed the rough ending of their marriage right out of the history books.

It didn't matter how cold it got out here, Grey had every intention of milking this snow fight for all it was worth. He hadn't been paying enough attention and got another snowball in the back of the head. He turned to find Dare grinning and giving Cora a thumbs up. Nice. He tossed Cora a mischievous smile before making a "T" with both of his hands.

"Okay, time out. Zac? You hear me, buddy? Time out. I have an idea."

He peeked cautiously around the tree, half expecting one of the kids to nail him with yet another snowball. It was a relief to see they'd come out, their faces full of curiosity. Cora and Dare came out into the open as well.

Mom was watching through the glass door on the porch. She'd come out earlier and taken several pictures and some video before retreating inside again where it was warm.

"What's your idea, Uncle Grey?" Zac fidgeted in the snow, barely containing his energy.

Grey paused for dramatic effect. "I think you and I should team up against Cora and Uncle Dare. We have ten minutes to make as many snowballs as we can and then have a huge finale of a snowball fight. What do you say?"

"Yeah!" Zac pumped his fist as a giant grin brightened his face. "We're gonna get you, Uncle Dare!"

Grey laughed hard at the boy's enthusiasm.

"We're in," Cora announced with Dare's nod of approval.

That daring look on her face had Grey wondering what she had up her sleeve. He noticed Zac, shivering a little, even if he didn't pay any attention himself. They wouldn't be able to stay out too much longer. "All right, then." He knuckle-bumped with Zac. "Let's do this."

Dare and Cora took off down the driveway and disappeared behind the snow-covered minivan that Flynn's family must have driven in.

"Come on, Zac." He waved his nephew around the side of the cabin. There, they spent ten minutes making as many snowballs as they could. Once time was up, they both armed themselves with as many as they could carry and then waited.

The sound of hesitant footsteps in the snow drew closer. Grey grasped a snowball in one hand, leaned around the corner, and let it fly. It landed right in the middle of Cora's stomach with a satisfying thud. Her mouth formed an "O" before she threw one in his direction. He ducked out of the way.

"Incoming!"

For the next fifteen minutes, the teams threw snowball after snowball until all four of them were covered with the evidence of their battle. Dare picked up Zac and held him above his head. Grey had one more snowball left and launched it at Cora. She dodged it and, with one sweeping motion, knocked his hat right off his head.

She took off running and ducked around the side of the minivan away from the cabin. Grey followed her at a full run. When he found her on the other side, she screamed and threw his hat at him to distract him and tried to get away.

He ignored the hat completely.

Instead, he dove for her, catching her around the waist and causing them both to land hard side by side in the snow.

Cora laughed, her breath mixing with the cold air to create little white clouds.

"Did you really think you'd get away with stealing my hat?" He lifted himself up on one elbow so he could look into her face.

"If it helps, it wasn't pre-meditated."

"Uh-huh." He raised an eyebrow at her. "You just had no choice but to grab it and run?"

She opened her mouth to say something, but shut it again and shrugged, her cheeks turning even redder then they already were from the cold.

In all the excitement of the snowball fight, most of the hair she'd carefully tucked under her winter hat had escaped. Strands of it framed her face, and there was no way he could stop himself from removing his glove and brushing the hair aside.

They both stilled the moment his hand touched her cheek. Her breath caught as he leaned in closer, drawn to her in a way he could no more control than the blizzard that had trapped them there in the first place. Her eyelashes fluttered twice before drifting closed.

His lips barely brushed against hers when the sound of Zac laughing had her pushing against his chest at the same time he was jumping away from her. He tried to cover his warring emotions over their near kiss by grabbing his hat and pulling it over his head, even though it was half-full of snow.

Dare and Zac rounded the corner. The little boy cheered. "Yeah! You got your hat back!" He ran forward and gave Grey a high five. "We won!" He proceeded to do a dance that had all three adults laughing.

"All right, little man, we need to get you inside before you turn into a Zac snowman," Dare told him. He shot Grey a look that insinuated he knew exactly what had been happening when they came around the van.

Cora dusted her jacked off. "You know what? I think we all deserve some hot chocolate. I'm pretty sure Grandma said there'd be some waiting for us when we went inside. What do you say?"

That was all Zac needed. He took off running and Dare raced him to the door leaving Grey and Cora to walk back together.

"There should seriously be a cap on that boy's energy," Cora said with a chuckle. "I'm so tired."

"But you had fun. Admit it, you enjoyed your first snowball fight." He glanced at her profile. Her response shouldn't matter, but it did. A lot.

"Yeah, I had fun." She gave him a shy smile.

They clomped up the steps and into the warm cabin. As Grey removed his wet boots, coat, hat, and gloves, he couldn't believe he'd nearly kissed Cora. The problem was, he couldn't decide if he was more relieved or disappointed that it'd been interrupted.

MARIA PUT water to heat over the fire in the main room. Cora happily helped her get mugs of hot chocolate for everyone who wanted some. Anything to get her mind off the fact that Grey had almost kissed her a few minutes ago.

She was going to let him, too. Cora suppressed a groan. Not only was she going to let him, but she was fully prepared to kiss him back.

It was a good thing Zac interrupted them, even if she'd felt a pang of disappointment when Grey had pulled away from her. Kissing Grey would open a whole box of trouble that she wasn't even willing to examine right now. The least of it was the mess of emotions it was bound to stir up.

Once they distributed the mugs of cocoa, Cora happily accepted one for herself. Everyone else was sitting in the main room, visiting or playing games as Cora and Maria walked in.

Maria gave a happy sigh. "Is it horrible that I don't even want the electricity to come back on?" She gave a little shrug. "This is just so peaceful. No one's got their attention on their cell phones or hiding out in front of the TV. For better or worse, we're forced to interact with each other. It's nice."

"It is nice." Cora took a sip of her hot chocolate. Grey's

eyes searched her face, an unspoken question on his own. There was an open spot next to him. Maria headed that way, so Cora sat on the hearth near Dare.

Cora pointed to the block of wood that Dare was still working on. It took several moments of studying it before she could really see what he was doing. "Wow, that's incredible." She reached a hand out. "May I?"

He nodded and gave it to her. He hadn't done much to the log, but there were little scenes carved into different places. Like windows into a memory. The one he'd already finished showed the fireplace, complete with a pot hanging over the fire and the firewood and poker on the hearth nearby. The scene he was working on now showed a kitchen table. Several types of food had already been added, but Cora suspected there were going to be more. "I don't know how you use a knife to get that much detail."

Dare shrugged as if it were no big deal and lowered his voice. "I figured I could make something to give Mom for Christmas. You know, something to remember this trip by." His ears reddened.

"I think that's a great idea. She'll love it." She handed the log back to him and then watched for a while as he continued to use his knife to carve details into the table.

A strange noise caught Cora's attention. With so many people in the room, she quickly dismissed it. But a moment later, she heard it again. Grey must have, too, because he stood, his eyes on the front door. He and Flynn exchanged glances.

"What is it, Daddy?" Zac asked.

"Most likely the wind. You just stay here, and we'll check it out."

Everyone was curious now as the two men approached the front door. Flynn pulled it open. They must not have seen anything at first because Grey pushed the screen door open. Immediately a mass of golden fur raced through the doorway, snow flying everywhere.

"A doggy!" Zac practically leaped off the floor only to be snatched up by his father.

"We don't know if the dog's nice or not, Zac."

The boy clearly didn't care. The dog, on the other hand, flew from person to person, tongue lapping at people's hands and faces as though it hadn't seen a living soul in weeks.

"Where did he come from?" Maria wondered.

"No clue," Grey responded, "but it was determined to get inside. The poor thing was probably freezing."

Cora grabbed the dog's collar as it bounded by her and pulled it to a stop. She bent down to look at its belly. His belly. "He looks like a full golden retriever, doesn't he?"

The dog used his front feet to hop up and down in excitement. Dare took his collar so Cora could let him go. "Yes, he does. No tags. What's your story, big guy?"

The dog woofed once as though answering. Everyone in the room chuckled.

"We can't let it stay here," Flynn objected. "What if someone's looking for it?"

Zac immediately threw his arms around the dog's neck and hugged it tight.

Flynn might be right, but just thinking about sending the poor guy back into the freezing cold made Cora sad. Who knew what he'd gone through to get to the cabin? "What if he's lost? No one's going to find him in this weather." Or even worse, what if the dog had nowhere to belong? That was a feeling she could certainly relate to at different times in her life.

Zac, at four years of age, already knew who to go to first. "Can he stay, Grandma? Please?"

Emma looked from her big brother to her grandmother and back again. "Peeese?"

Abby put a hand over her mouth but there was no missing the way her shoulders shook with laughter.

Maria and Flynn exchanged a look that said it all. Flynn stood and reached for the dog's collar. "Let's take him into the kitchen, get him some food and water, and we'll go from there."

The kids cheered so loudly that the dog lifted his ears and barked again.

Cora followed the crowd into the kitchen and watched as the dog wolfed down the half sandwich that was left over from lunch. He drank a bunch of water, dripping some of it on the floor as he turned to look longingly at the counter. When Maria picked up another slice of sandwich meat, the dog again bounced up and down on his front legs.

"What are we gonna name him?" Zac asked.

"Well, we do need to call him something," Mom agreed. She looked thoughtful. "How about Pogo?"

Laughter and approving comments filled the room.

Zac looked up at his dad. "Can we keep him, Dad? Please?"

Flynn shook his head firmly. "Someone probably misses him, buddy. Once we have power, we'll call down to the resort and see if someone is looking for him. If so, I'm sure they'll be really glad we found him and gave him some food."

The little boy nodded sadly. Cora felt for him. She'd never had a pet as a child. Her parents had insisted that they were too dirty and too much work. No matter how many times Cora promised to take care of it herself, the answer was always "no."

As if the dog could sense her thoughts, he walked through

everyone else and sat down at her feet. Cora crouched on the floor beside him and ran her hand over his head. She'd always wanted a dog, and Pogo here would be perfect. Too bad the timing was all wrong.

Grey moved to stand next to her. "If we can't find the owner, you should take him home with you. I bet he'd be a great guard dog."

"Maybe. But I work twelve-hour shifts at the hospital. I can tell just by looking at Pogo that he needs a lot of attention and opportunities to run. He'd be miserable waiting for me to come home. Probably make the neighbors miserable." She doubted her apartment building would even let her have a dog that large in the first place. "Maybe you could take him home. He could be your store's mascot."

Grey seemed to consider the idea. If he took Pogo, she could always go by the store to see him.

The dog, not Grey.

Not that she had any intention of going by Grey's store for any reason.

The fact the idea had popped into her mind at all annoyed Cora. That near kiss had obviously messed with her brain more than she'd thought.

CHAPTER ELEVEN

G rey had been playing poker with Dare, Mom, and
Cora at the kitchen table when a blood curdling
scream drew everyone to the living room. They found Zac
standing near the fire place, the log Dare had been working
on at his feet, and blood dripping from his left hand. Pogo
was whining at him, clearly concerned.

Abby reached the boy first, but only by moments. She
nudged the dog out of the way and knelt in front of her son.
Dare led Pogo off to the side so he wouldn't get in the middle
of everything.

Once Grey got closer, it was clear what had happened
when they all saw the open pocket knife lying on the ground
near the log.

Flynn's back straightened. "Zac, I've told you a hundred
times not to mess with pocket knives unless someone's
helping you."

Abby gave him a surprised look. "He cut himself really
bad. I think that's punishment enough."

Flynn raised a challenging eyebrow at Dare. "Maybe if
certain people didn't just leave their knives lying around..."

After his less-than-veiled accusation, he handed Emma to Mom and then turned his attention to his son. Abby held Zac's hand in hers as blood continued to drip. The boy cried even though he couldn't seem to take his eyes off the wound.

Dare's eyes flashed. "I get you're worried about your son, Flynn. But maybe you should do some checking before you start throwing accusations around." He patted his pocket. "My knife is right here."

Flynn bent to retrieve the knife on the ground then grunted. "Zac, did you go upstairs and get my knife off the side table?"

Zac's chin dropped as he stared at something invisible on the floor.

In true Flynn fashion, he ignored the fact that he owed Dare an apology. Grey would've said something if it weren't for Zac's finger.

"This is really deep, Flynn."

Grey's older brother knelt next to his son and nodded grimly.

"I'd be happy to take a look if you want me to." Cora's voice brought everyone's attention to the back of the crowd. "I even brought my medical bag with me—I don't go anywhere without it. I'm sure we can get his hand fixed up in no time."

Abby hesitated only a moment before moving so Cora could get closer. Flynn didn't argue, but it was clear he was less than happy about this turn of events. Grey wagered that if it'd been Flynn's own hand, he'd have used a staple gun or duct tape before he would've let Cora help.

Zac buried his hand in his shirt and shook his head, adamant that Cora wasn't going to touch him. Blood from his finger had already smeared across the front of his shirt.

Cora sat cross legged on the floor and patted the rug next

to her. Zac sat too, looking wary. "I'm going to go get my medical bag. When I bring it down, do you think you can help me? I have a stethoscope you can use to listen to your own heartbeat. What do you say?" Zac only hesitated a moment or two before he finally nodded. "Wonderful! But I need to look at your hand first, just so I know what size bandage to bring down in my bag. Do you think I can do that? I promise I won't touch it right now."

Zac held his shaky hand out and opened it to reveal a cut on his thumb. It wasn't more than an inch long, but even Grey could see how it was split open from his vantage point.

Cora gave him a kind smile. "Good job, buddy. Okay, hold it against your shirt again and wait right here. I'll go get my bag, and we'll see if we can find that stethoscope."

She stepped away and headed for the stairs. Pogo broke away from Dare to lope after her while Grey jogged to catch up. Once they were out of earshot, he said, "Zac's going to need some stitches, isn't he?"

"Maybe. But I think I can use a butterfly bandage and some glue to close the wound."

"Let me guess, you have everything you need in your bag?"

Cora grinned at him as she opened the door to her room. "There was a legitimate reason why my suitcase was so heavy." The playful wink she gave him made his heart stutter.

Pogo jumped onto the bed and watched as she rummaged through her suitcase until she produced a large, leather bag with a shoulder strap. "You're not the only one that goes everywhere prepared."

"Thank goodness for that." Grey watched as she retrieved a towel and a washcloth from the bathroom.

When they got downstairs, Zac was still sitting on the

floor, clearly hurting. Cora motioned for Flynn and Abby to join her. Mom patted Emma on the back and walked to the window to talk about what they saw outside.

"Zac's going to need more than a bandage to close that cut, but I don't think stitches are going to be necessary. Since I don't have a good way to numb the skin first, I'd rather avoid that anyway. I can use a butterfly bandage and some glue to fix it. Are you both okay with that?"

Flynn and Abby looked at each other a moment before nodding.

Once she had permission, Cora sat down in front of Zac and gave him a reassuring smile. "Let's see if I can find my stethoscope. Did you know this bag has so many things in it, it may as well not have a bottom?"

Zac's eyes widened as she made an exaggerated search through her bag.

"Ah, here we are." Cora withdrew the stethoscope from her bag and helped Zac listen to his own heart.

The boy's worried face broke into a smile. Then he pointed to the bag with his uninjured hand. "What else?"

"I'm going to show you. But first, I need to tell you something. You know that cut on your thumb? A bandage isn't going to be enough to help it get better. Have you ever watched your dad fix something that's broken by using glue?" Zac nodded. "That's exactly what I need to do for you. I have some magic glue that'll fix your thumb all up." She tickled his side a little and managed to get a giggle out of him. Pogo joined them then, lying on the floor with his chin resting on Zac's shoe.

"Wow, Cora's really good at what she does, isn't she?" Dare's voice held a measure of awe.

"Yes, she is." When she'd told Grey she was a registered

nurse, he had no doubt she was good at her job. But watching her in action was a whole different thing. Even though Zac was worried and hurting, she had him trusting her to make him better.

He pictured her tending to their own child had things gone differently. Cora would've been an amazing mom. He tried to push the image aside, unprepared for the way it made his heart trip inside his chest.

Truthfully, every time he thought he might be getting serious about a woman he was dating, he'd picture their future together. When he did that, it was like staring into a thick fog. Unlike when he was dating Cora. Back then, he'd had no doubt where their relationship was heading. The inability to see that with anyone else was more than frustrating.

It didn't take long for Cora to clean Zac's wound, pull the skin together, and apply glue to keep everything in place. Once she'd finished, she put antibiotic cream and a bandage on his thumb.

"There we go. Now that wasn't so bad, was it?"

Zac shook his head. He held his thumb up for everyone to see, a big grin on his face.

Abby gave her son a big hug. "Come on, sweetie. Why don't we go upstairs, get you a clean shirt, and then I'll find you some Tylenol in our bathroom bag." She smiled at Cora before leading Zac to the stairs. "Thank you."

"Of course. I'm glad I could help."

Flynn retrieved Emma from Mom's arms, gave Cora a nod, and followed the rest of his family.

Dare hooked an arm around Cora's shoulders. "And that, my dear, is about as close as you'll get to a thank you from Flynn." He dropped his arm and laughed.

Mom started to clean the blood off the floor. Thankfully nearly all of it had landed on the tile and not on the rug.

Cora packed the rest of her stuff back into her bag and stood. She rolled her shoulders and tilted her head to one side, causing her neck to pop. "That's better."

Grey just nearly reached out to rub her neck and shoulders but stopped himself. It was exactly what he would've done when they were married, and the fact that he'd nearly instinctively done so both amazed and bothered him.

"Is it ready?" Zac could hardly stand still. Abby helped him keep his metal coat hanger and marshmallow hovering just above the fire.

When Maria came into the living room bearing marshmallows, graham crackers, chocolate bars, and plenty of metal roasters, Zac was immediately excited.

Truthfully, Cora was right there with him. She'd had her first s'mores when she went camping with Grey and his family. It was something her own parents never would've splurged on.

Sitting around the campfire with the Jackson family— roasting marshmallows and trying to eat the sticky treats— was one of her favorite memories.

It also happened to be one of her most memorable kisses with Grey. He'd softly touched her chin with his finger, whispered that she had a little marshmallow on the corner of her mouth, and proceeded to kiss it away.

Just remembering it sent chills racing up and down Cora's spine.

Things were very different this time. There would be no kiss. No promise of future campouts together.

But there was chocolate. If there was one thing Cora learned long ago, it's that you should never underestimate the power of chocolate when it comes to making things better.

Cora threaded a large marshmallow onto her roaster and held it over the flame in the fireplace. It was dark outside, and the flames were the only source of light in the living room.

Even Pogo seemed interested in what everyone else was doing. Grey tossed the dog a marshmallow, and they laughed as he chewed repeatedly. They weren't sure he was even going to eat it, but before long, he was begging for another.

After Cora finished her second s'more, she set her roasting stick on the hearth and went to sit down. Most of the furniture was already being used. She went to the large over-stuffed recliner and arrived just as Abby did. She had a sleepy Emma in her arms. Cora motioned to the chair. "You go ahead."

"Thank you. She's been yawning for a while. I don't think it'll take her long to go to sleep." She got comfortable, and little Emma yawned again with her head resting against her mom's chest.

Cora ended up sitting on the rug with her back to the bricks of the large hearth. A moment later, Grey joined her.

The family began to relate their favorite stories about Grandpa Jackson. There was a lot of laughter and joking. Even Flynn, who held Zac on his lap, looked content for the first time that weekend.

Cora's heart ached. She was completely unaware she'd been crying until Grey gently wiped a tear from her cheek. He didn't ask her if she was okay or say anything at all.

Thoughts swirled around in her head until she finally whispered to Grey, "I wish we knew whether our baby was a boy or a girl."

"I felt like it was a girl from the very beginning," he said with conviction. "She would've looked just like you."

"She should be here right now." She was on the verge of losing control of her emotions. She bit her lip to keep the tears at bay and tried to sniff discreetly.

Grey didn't say a word. Instead, he put an arm around her shoulders and drew her close to his side. It meant more than anything he might have voiced. For once, Cora didn't care what the others thought, or even if it meant it might complicate things between them later. What she needed was support and comfort from the only person who knew what she was feeling right now.

This time, when their hands brushed, she didn't hesitate to place hers in his. Their fingers laced together without a second thought from Cora.

Suddenly, the lights flickered on, effectively blinding everyone. Cora flinched and closed her eyes. She wasn't sure who let go first, but their hands fell away from each other and cooler air seeped into the new space between them.

Zac stood and jumped around with excitement. The hum of the heater announced that soon, the entire cabin would be warm again.

"Finally." Flynn stood and brushed off his pants. "I'm going to get my cell phone and charge it. Hopefully we can call someone at the resort or the airport and get an update." He began to go upstairs.

Abby grabbed her son's arm as he ran by. "Zac, your sister is asleep. I need you to quiet down a little."

He looked at Emma and sat down again, properly chastised. Emma stirred a little before snuggling closer to Abby.

Maria stood, too. She made an exaggerated sad expression. "I guess that's it." She almost looked lost as she took in the lit interior of the cabin.

Cora got up from her spot on the floor and gave her a hug. "No, it's not. We still have tonight." She tried to give Maria a smile of encouragement, but she felt it, too. It felt as if the lights coming on had burst this bubble they'd all been living in. Now real life would creep back in, and she wasn't sure she was ready for it.

CHAPTER TWELVE

Grey knew people's priorities might shift once the electricity came on. To see Flynn, though, you'd think the cabin was on fire and he had to do everything he could to get out at that very moment. He was on the phone and pacing back and forth between the dining room and living room.

Abby put the kids to bed. Now that the electricity was on, they didn't have to light a fire in the room, and Emma was in the portable crib. Abby brought the baby monitor downstairs so she could listen in case either of the kids got up. She kept looking at Flynn anxiously as he continued to pace.

Cora was nestled into one corner of the couch, Pogo lying on the floor at her feet, while Dare sat at the opposite end. Grey finally plopped down between them. He looked over at Mom who was sitting in the recliner with an afghan spread out over her lap. The corners of her mouth pulled down a bit and there was a sadness in her eyes.

Flynn ended the call and stuffed the phone in his back pocket. "I just spoke to someone who said the airport is back up and running, and that they're going to try to get everyone's flights swapped around so people can get home as soon as possible. But there's no guarantee that we'd get a flight tomorrow, or if it's going to be Tuesday." He turned to look at Abby, desperation oozing from his pores. "It's going to be first come, first served. I wish we could get the kids and try to make it down there tonight."

Dare blinked in surprise. "That's not a good idea, man. The roads between here and there are as treacherous as they were before the electricity came on."

Cora nodded. "Remember, Grey and I couldn't even make it halfway here because the roads were so bad. I know you're in a hurry to get home, but if you get stuck out there some-where in the middle of the night—"

Flynn whirled and fixed her with a stern look that bordered on anger. "Just because you patched up Zac's finger doesn't mean we're good here, Cora. I suggest you stay out of my family's business."

Cora stood from the couch, her brows drawn together and her hands in fists. "I've put up with a lot from you over the years, Flynn. Listen to yourself! Who are you to lecture me about staying out of someone else's business? Did it ever occur to you that you may have had a small part in the avalanche that led to what happened to Grey and me?"

Now it was Grey's turn to be surprised. He looked from one of them to the other. "What are you talking about, Cora?" He knew Flynn had been less than supportive of their marriage, but this seemed to be something else. When neither of them replied, he stood. "Cora?"

Cora stared at Flynn as though daring him to tell them first. When he said nothing, she finally took a breath and turned to look at Grey. "Flynn came by the house one evening while you were traveling. There was a lot of tension between the two of us, and everyone in the family knew it. He told me it was all happening just like he said it would, and that I was responsible for your unhappiness." Her voice broke as she stared at Flynn. "I knew better than to listen to you, but I wasn't exactly full of self-esteem back then."

Flynn didn't deny her words.

"Flynn Carson!" Mom's voice spoke of her shock and disappointment.

By now, Abby's face was filled with a combination of dread and embarrassment. "Flynn, maybe we should go get some sleep..." She reached for his hand.

Flynn held it gently but kept his gaze locked with Grey's. "You go ahead, Abby. I'll be up in a few minutes."

The poor woman only stood next to him, unsure what to do.

It took everything Grey had to keep his own hands at his sides. "You had no right to go to our house and talk to my wife like that. If I'd known..."

Mom jumped up then and stood between them. "This isn't the way to solve anything." She pivoted to face Flynn. "This is our last night here. Why are you ruining it like this? What's so important that you're talking about trying to get to the airport tonight? You should listen to Cora and Grey. It's not safe."

Flynn's ears turned red. He looked Grey in the eyes. "You and Cora have no idea what it's like to take care of a family, to make sure the kids have proper insurance, food on the table, and clothes on their backs. When you've had some of that worry, you come talk to me." He was still holding Abby's hand when he turned toward the stairs.

Cora took two steps forward and planted her hands on her hips. "You have no idea what you're talking about." Her voice was wrapped in anger as she crossed her arms in front of her. She glanced back at Grey as though asking for permission. His nod gave it to her.

She started to speak and her voice broke. She cleared her throat and tried again. "We were going to have a baby, Grey and I. We were planning to announce it at Christmas, but it ended up being an ectopic pregnancy."

There were tears in her voice now. Grey moved to stand beside her and reached for her hand. He met Flynn's eyes. "Her tube burst, and they had to perform emergency surgery to save Cora's life. She was so upset and worried. Between the little support she got from her parents, and you, she thought it would be better if we didn't tell anyone."

He saw Mom put a hand over her mouth as a tear rolled down her cheek.

Grey wasn't done yet. He pointed a finger at Flynn. "We may not have had the experience of raising kids like you have, but I know what it's like to lose my child and nearly lose my wife. Don't talk to me about what it takes to care for your family, to pay off hospital bills."

Cora took a shaky breath. "That night you came over and said those things, Flynn, I was still recovering from the surgery. I was already feeling all kinds of guilt over not being able to give Grey our child." Her voice broke again and this time, she covered her face with her hands.

Grey had no idea she'd felt that way. He stepped in front of her and put a hand on each of her shoulders. "I never blamed you. Not once." She only nodded. A moment later, she turned away and raced up the stairs with Pogo following on her heels. He was going to go after her, but Mom stopped him.

"Let me, Grey." She shook her head at Flynn. "I don't even know what to say to you right now." With that, she followed Cora.

Dare got to his feet and stalked across the room to the fireplace and back again.

Truthfully, Grey would've decked Flynn more than once if it hadn't been for Abby. He had no intention of doing that in front of her. His thoughts shifted to Cora, and he wondered if he should go find her anyway.

The four of them stood there for several minutes until Mom came back downstairs. She nodded to Grey. "She's going to be okay. She opted to go to bed, and I can't say as I blame her." She regained her spot in the recliner and stared at her oldest.

Abby stood on tip-toes and whispered something in her husband's ear. He looked like he was going to argue before his shoulders finally dropped. This time it was his turn to sit on the hearth. Abby joined him. "I need to get back home before tomorrow afternoon because I have an interview." He paused. "I was fired from my previous employer two months ago and have been finding it difficult to locate a new job." From the sound of his voice, it was near torture to have to utter those words.

Grey knew it was hard for any man to admit what Flynn just had. But for Flynn, it was even more so, seeing as he was one of the most prideful men Grey had ever known. He understood now why Flynn so desperately needed to get back in time, but even if they got to the airport first thing in the morning and flights were figured out by noon, it'd be a miracle if Flynn and his family made it home in time.

Dare was the first one to speak. "You were stuck in a true blizzard. Now that you have cell phone service, you can call the company you're interviewing with tomorrow morning and explain that. I'll bet they can reschedule your interview."

"Maybe." Flynn looked doubtful. "But I need this job, and it wasn't easy to get the interview lined up in the first place." He ran a hand over his face. "Look, I think we're going to call it a night, and we'll see if we can get things figured out in the morning. Who knows? Maybe they'll clear the roads first thing and we'll have a shot at getting out of here early." He did, at least, have the good sense to give Mom a look of contrition. "I'm sorry."

"So am I." Mom's voice was quiet. "I'm sorry that people in this family feel like they have to hide things from each other instead of relying on each other for help." She sounded sad.

Flynn kissed her on the cheek, took Abby's hand, and the two of them went upstairs.

Now that it was just Grey, Dare, and Mom, the living room seemed huge and empty. They sat staring at the fire that continued to crackle and burn in the hearth.

CORA COULDN'T SLEEP. She was still angry at Flynn, upset with herself for losing her temper like she did, and completely spent after such an emotional admission downstairs. She had to admit, though, that it felt better to have finally told everyone about the baby. A tightness in her chest seemed to finally ease a little.

She'd processed her emotions surrounding the loss of the baby, but all this tonight had opened that back up again. Everything felt raw.

A half hour later, she finally gave up trying to sleep. Redressing, she slowly made her way down the hall and partway down the stairs. She'd tried to leave Pogo in her room, but he'd have none of it. Rather than risk him barking and waking the kids up, she motioned for him to follow.

There was no sign of Flynn or Abby, but Dare, Grey, and Maria were still sitting in the living room.

One of the stairs creaked bringing Grey's attention to her. He got to his feet as his face filled with concern. She wrapped her arms around her waist.

"Can't sleep?" Mom asked. Cora shook her head. "I can't imagine why not." Mom offered her a small smile. "You know, we do still have plenty of chocolate bars left over from making s'mores. I don't know about the rest of you, but I could go for a good chocolate fix about now."

Cora couldn't agree more. Grey waited for her to sit down on the couch before doing the same.

Maria returned and handed out the candy bars. The room was filled with the sounds of the wrappers being opened.

Cora snapped off a piece of chocolate and let it melt on her tongue. Yep, chocolate really did make everything better. They ate in companionable silence for a while.

Dare finished his chocolate first and crumpled the wrapper in one hand. He looked at Cora. "Were you able to get a hold of someone at the hospital?"

"Yes, thank you. My friend, Jen, had left me several texts asking me to call her the moment I could to check in. I talked to her for a few minutes, then called into the hospital. They were able to bring in another nurse for my shift in the morning."

Jen had asked Cora how things were going, and it took everything in Cora to keep control of her emotions. She promised to tell Jen all the news once she got back. And this time, she'd tell her about the ectopic pregnancy as well.

Cora realized she'd been staring at the fire without seeing it, a piece of chocolate held between her thumb and finger. It'd started to melt. She put it in her mouth and then licked the chocolate residue as well. "What about the rest of you? Did you get a hold of anyone?"

Dare propped his sock-covered feet on the coffee table. "I'm waiting until first thing in the morning. I was afraid that calling too late would get me fired as well. Trying to find that happy balance." It was said with sarcasm, but he had a smile on his face. "My boss isn't going to like that I'm calling in last minute, but at least I won't be a no-show."

"I hope your boss understands," Cora said. She looked at Grey and Maria. "I suppose you both have to wait until your stores are open to check in, too."

Maria nodded. "I do, but my manager has been working for me for years. There was no voicemail from him, so I'm confident all is well."

"Same here." Grey finished the last bite of his chocolate. "Brody has things under control."

They all visited for several more minutes before Maria stood and said she thought she was finally ready to go to sleep. Dare agreed. They both gave her a hug and left. She wasn't sure if they really were ready to go to bed, or if they felt like she and Grey needed some time to talk. Either way, she welcomed the quiet.

Grey moved to the hearth and worked on banking the fire. "I almost hate to put it out completely. We may want another one in the morning."

Cora nodded. The central heating had effectively warmed up the entire cabin, but there was nothing better than a fire on a cold morning. Especially on a morning that was full of unknowns as tomorrow was bound to be.

She stood, watching, as Grey worked. When he'd finished, he returned the poker and turned to face her.

"I'm sorry, Cora."

She blinked at him in surprise. "What on earth for?"

"I should've been there when Flynn came by that night. I never should've left on a picking trip until you'd completely recovered from the surgery." He released a heavy sigh. "I was stupid and clueless."

"We both were, Grey. We were both young, confused, and dealing with a lot. I should have told you or asked you to stay. I should've confronted Flynn at the time instead of letting him get the best of my self-confidence." All of those were things she'd agonized over for years. This was the first time, though, that thinking about them didn't immediately fill her with regret or anger. If nothing else resulted from this week-end, being free of some of that made the trip worthwhile. Although if she didn't have to deal with drama for a while, that would be great.

She didn't realize she'd started to smile until Grey returned it. "What?"

"It felt good to finally tell Flynn what I thought of him." She laughed and then covered her mouth and looked toward the stairs. It was doubtful anyone could hear them, but she had to remember they weren't alone in the cabin.

"I know exactly what you mean." He sobered. "I do hope he can get the interview rescheduled, though."

"I do, too."

They were both silent again for several moments. Cora's eyes suddenly felt tired and heavy.

Grey gave her another little smile. "We should go get some sleep. Tomorrow's going to be a busy day. With any luck, we'll be back in our own places by this time tomorrow."

Cora ought to be relieved about that, but going their separate ways also meant losing touch with Grey again. The thought depressed her. "Who knows? Maybe we'll end up on the same plane back to DFW."

"You never know." Grey took several steps toward her

before stopping. "You asked if I thought we'd given up too easily."

Cora nodded, her gaze transfixed on his face.

"I don't know about that, but I do know that if I could go back in time, I'd do things differently."

CHAPTER THIRTEEN

All Grey could hear was the hum of the heater and the sound of his own heart beating in his ear. He meant what he said about doing things differently. "I would've stayed home more. I never would've left you while you were still recovering from your surgery."

Cora looked hesitant as she pulled her lower lip in between her teeth; a quirk that always drove him to distraction. Even now, it made him want to kiss her until every worry faded away.

She nodded, her gaze finally settling on his face. "I would have done things differently, too. I don't know that it would've changed the ending to our story, but at least I wouldn't have so many regrets." Her voice broke.

Grey took another step closer. He slowly studied her face, from her expressive eyes down to her red lips and back again. Before he gave himself a chance to analyze what he was feeling, or talk himself out of it, he lowered his head and allowed his lips to gently caress hers. That kiss was their only point of contact until Cora's hand traveled across his shoulder and rested on the back of his neck.

He wrapped his arm around her waist, drawing her closer and deepening the kiss. Everything else faded away. In that moment, there was no worrying about getting on a plane tomorrow, or what it might mean once they got back home. There was no divorce. In that moment, there was only holding Cora and marveling at how *right* it felt, more so than anything he'd experienced since they'd gone their separate ways.

When their kiss ended, he placed another to her forehead.

She pressed her palms against his chest. "Grey…"

And the doubt in her voice brought all those things that had faded away crashing back into the room with them. He knew everything she was going to say, and his own doubts only echoed them back.

Cora took a step backwards. "I can't do this." She looked at him then, her eyes pleading for him to understand. "*We* can't do this. Not again."

Grey wanted to argue with her but said nothing for several moments. Finally, he took in a deep breath and ran his fingers through his hair. "Common sense tells me that you're right." He reached for her hand. "But I don't want to go through the rest of my life wondering if it might have turned out differently if we'd only given us another shot."

His words brought tears to her eyes. "And if we fail? I don't know that I can go through losing us again. Grey, those first two years after the divorce were horrible. I lost my best friend, my husband, and the only real family I ever had." She sniffed. "This weekend was wonderful in many ways, but it was also a reminder of what I don't have any more. I can't step into that world only to have it crumble out from under me again."

Grey's chest ached. "I don't want to add another notch to

the regret list, and I think walking away from each other will do just that."

"Then where does that leave us?" The words were spoken sadly as she withdrew her hand from his and buried it in her pocket.

Grey's mind struggled to make sense of their situation. In that moment, he knew Dare had been right. Grey was still very much in love with his ex-wife. The only thing he was certain of was that if he let her go now, it would prove to be one of the biggest mistakes he could make.

"Maybe we failed at marriage," he began, "but I think this weekend has proved that we still have a connection."

He paused, and when she didn't deny his words, it bolstered his courage to continue.

"I have it on good authority that our friendship truce will remain in effect even across state lines. In fact, it's even more effective in Texas than it is in Colorado. Or so I've heard."

The sadness in her eyes gave way to a flicker of humor. She crossed her arms in front of her. "And I'm pretty sure the friendship truce does *not* include what just happened here moments ago."

He wanted to point out that there'd been many, many times in the past when he'd kissed her, his best friend, and quite thoroughly. But he didn't think it'd help build his case now, so he kept that thought to himself.

"So, if we add in a no kissing clause to the friendship truce, you might consider extending it?" He tried to act casual while he was desperately hoping and praying for her to agree.

Grey wished he could get even a tiny view into what she was thinking as she seemed to mull over his words.

Cora finally gave a definitive nod. "Yes."

That one word had him breathing a sigh of relief. Maybe

it wasn't exactly what he was hoping for, but it was a new beginning. They had to start somewhere.

"In that case, I'll bid you good night. See you tomorrow, friend."

"Good night, Grey."

Her smile was the last thing he saw as she started up the stairs and disappeared into the darkness.

CORA STARED at her reflection in the bathroom mirror. Being held in Grey's arms was one of the most amazing, and most confusing, things she'd ever experienced. A big part of her wanted to stay there and pretend like the rest of the world didn't exist.

For a few brief moments, she'd even been able to imagine all was right between them, and that they'd never had to sign those divorce papers or say goodbye.

But all of that did happen, and her heart ached with the memories. Living through it once had been nightmare enough. She didn't think she could open herself up to going through it a second time, and especially not with Grey. Not after being reminded of what they used to have together.

She wasn't so naïve as to believe that his suggestion of extending their friendship truce was an easy solution. At the same time, she couldn't risk losing everything again, and she didn't want to let go of what they'd managed to recover over the weekend.

Cora yawned and crawled into bed with a sigh. Being friends was a good compromise. Their amazing kiss earlier came to mind again. It would be a good compromise as long as they didn't keep doing *that*.

"Please keep us from messing this up too," she prayed. As

her eyelids fell, the emotional storm of the day faded away into blissful sleep.

The next thing she knew, sunshine was spilling through her window. She woke slowly until the smell of bacon wafted under the door to her room and had her stomach growling in moments. The thought of a warm breakfast inspired her to dress in record time. Pogo waited at the door of her room, probably just as drawn to the amazing smells, too. As they descended the stairs, music reached Cora's ears.

Travis Tritt's song, "Anymore" pulled her into the kitchen. She crossed the threshold to find Maria dancing with Grey. Dare was grinning as the music continued to play from his phone. He glanced up when Cora walked into the room.

"Hey! My dance partner finally arrived." He set the phone on the counter before holding his hand out with a smile.

Cora chuckled as she placed her hand in his and let him sweep her into a dance. "What is all of this?" she asked above the music.

Maria's face was joyful as she said, "Dare created a playlist of Grandpa Jackson's favorite songs."

Dare shrugged. "After last night, I thought we could all do with a reminder of why we'd come here in the first place."

"That's a great idea." Flynn's voice from the doorway had all four of them stopping in their tracks. It was difficult to know what to expect after everything the night before. In his arms, he held little Emma, who was rubbing her eyes as she took in the scene.

Maria brightened as she stepped away from Grey and reached for her granddaughter. "Come here, sweetie. Come dance with Grandma." Emma wrapped her little arms around Maria's neck as she swayed to the music.

"I wanna dance!" Zac flew into the kitchen, a tornado of energy.

Dare winked at Cora and turned to the boy. "Come here, buddy. Let's show them how it's done."

Abby entered then, a smile on her face. "Well, isn't this fun to wake up to." She gave a little yelp when Flynn took her hand, made her twirl, and then began to dance with her.

Grey moved to stand beside Cora. "I guess that leaves you and me. Would you care to dance?"

The hopeful look on his face, and the laughter and smiles of everyone around her, quickly diffused her hesitation. As his arm went around her waist and his hand closed over hers, Cora's pulse sped up.

There was no doubt about it: being in his arms affected her in a way nothing else could. Less than a day into their renewed friendship truce and already she was having to curb her reactions. She reminded herself that it would be easier once they returned to real life.

They'd barely started dancing when the song ended, and another began. The moment George Strait's "All My Ex's Live in Texas" came on, the room filled with laughter. Grey's chuckle reached her ears as he said for all to hear, "I'm just glad I only have one."

Cora's face warmed, and she let her forehead rest against Grey's chest to hide what she knew was the start of an embarrassing blush. When she finally looked up into his green eyes, she found amusement and an echo of something else she used to see in his eyes years ago.

The oven timer went off, and Cora welcomed the interruption. She stepped out of his arms to help Maria finish breakfast preparations.

Fifteen minutes later, they all sat around the dining room table with plates full of scrambled eggs, bacon, and fresh biscuits.

There was very little talking as everyone enjoyed the

meal. Maria wiped her hand on her napkin and looked around the table. "Thank you for this morning. It means a lot," she said with a watery smile. "So, what is our plan of attack?"

Cora admired Maria for being able to transition into getting ready to go. With any luck, the roads would be plowed sometime this morning. It was a good idea to do what they could to be prepared.

Flynn was the first to speak up. "I thought we guys could start shoveling out the cars."

Grey nodded. "Agreed. Then we'll make sure everything is packed and ready to bring downstairs. That way, when the snowplows do come through, we'll be ready to load the vehicles and get going." He set his fork down. "Cora and I are going to need a ride."

"We'll have you covered," Dare assured him.

With their goals in mind, everyone focused on finishing breakfast. Afterward, Cora helped Maria with the dishes. Then they worked to put all the food into the fridge again now that the electricity was running. They heard the front door open followed by Dare calling out, "Cora? You downstairs?"

She and Maria exchanged a worried glance and ran into the living room. All three of the guys had returned from digging out the vehicles. Flynn and Dare were on either side of Grey, both offering support as Grey hobbled forward on one leg. A red stain radiated from a tear in his jeans just below the knee.

"What happened?" Maria followed them to the dining room where they eased Grey into a chair.

Cora retrieved several towels from the kitchen and returned in time to hear Dare's explanation.

"We needed another shovel. Grey volunteered to go find one."

"And I did." He lifted his leg for emphasis then cringed. "Apparently someone left one lying by the side of the cabin before all the snow hit. I tripped over the handle and landed on the edge of the shovel."

Cora cringed and looked at Dare. "Would you mind grabbing my medical bag from my room? It's on the dresser."

"Sure thing."

She knelt on the floor, towels in hand. "Let's see what we've got here." In full nurse mode, Cora pulled the torn fabric apart so she could see the wound inside. "Wow, they must have sharpened that shovel." She dabbed at his skin with the towel to clear away some blood. "This could've been a lot worse. You'll need stitches, but it didn't nick an artery."

Dare returned then and set her bag down beside her. "Here you go."

"Thank you." She dug in her kit for the pair of scissors she knew always fell toward the bottom. Using them, she cut away his pants leg to see the wound better. "I need to clean it." She lifted the bottle of alcohol to show him and knew it was going to be very painful. "You ready?"

"Just do it." Grey hissed as she poured the liquid over the cut. "Dare?"

"Yeah, man?"

"Next time you go get the snow shovel."

That had everyone chuckling, which eased the tension in the room. If there was one thing Cora had learned from working in the ER, it was that a sense of humor was vital. She smiled when the three brothers started to rib each other about who had received the worst injury growing up.

While they compared broken limbs and busted lips, Cora cleaned up the wound. It was bleeding less but was going to require four or five stitches to close it. "I can sew it up, Grey, but all I have is a topical numbing agent. If you want, I can bandage this, and we can see if the airport has a medical area that's better equipped."

Grey immediately shook his head. "They're going to be overtaxed as it is after this blizzard. They may not have any more supplies than you do. The topical will be fine. Let's just get this done so these jokers," he pointed to his brothers, "can finish digging the cars out."

Cora didn't have to ask him if he was sure, she could see the determination on his face. "You got it."

Abby and the kids came downstairs. Abby went to wait with Maria and Emma while Zac, on the other hand, happily sat on his daddy's lap to watch. "Cool!" He held his thumb out. "Just like me."

Grey chuckled. "Yep, we'll match." Then he gave Cora a nod to let her know he was ready.

"I'll need you to sit on the floor. Can someone grab a pillow for him to lean against, please?" There was a time in the past when Cora would've been all nerves working like this in front of the entire family. Now, however, she was able to push all that to the back of her mind and focus on the task in front of her.

While someone retrieved the pillow, Cora put a towel on the floor beneath Grey's leg. Then she opened one of the large, sterile pads and laid that on top of the towel. She opened a sealed package that contained some gloves and put them on. His wound was oozing a steady trickle of blood. She cleaned it again then used gauze to wipe the area clear. Before blood could cover the skin again, she applied iodine all around the cut including a good six inches in any direction. "Okay, that's going to make this as sterile as I can. Now, this lidocaine will numb the skin some."

Cora met his eyes to let him know it was still going to

hurt as she stitched. He nodded his understanding. She applied the lidocaine, waited for it to take effect, and began.

With each stitch, the blood flow lessened until the wound was finally closed. She used some more iodine to rinse the area and alcohol wipes to clean the rest of his leg, including the trails the blood had left behind. When she was done, she dried the wound with gauze before applying more and wrapping it with a stretchy bandage to keep it in place.

"All right, there we go." She pulled her gloves off, turning them inside out in the process. "I've got acetaminophen in here. Would you like some?"

Grey flexed his leg, accepted help from Dare and Flynn, and got to his feet. "I think that may not be a bad idea."

Maria appeared moments later with a glass of water. Grey swallowed the medication while Cora cleaned up the towel and trash.

Dare put an arm around her shoulders. "That was impressive, Cora. Remind me to bring you along on all of our excursions." He was teasing her, but his expression was serious.

"It's not a big deal." Now that she was done, and everyone was either thanking her or watching her with awe, she felt her cheeks warm. "I'm just glad I could help, and that it wasn't any worse." She turned to Grey. "You should probably see a doctor when you get home, though. Have it looked at and maybe even get some antibiotics to make sure you don't get an infection."

"I'll keep that in mind." He leaned forward then, and Cora thought he was going to kiss her cheek, but he stopped and smiled instead. "Thank you."

"You're welcome." If her cheeks hadn't been warm before, they were practically on fire now. "Just watch those snow shovels in the future, huh?"

He grinned. "Yes, ma'am."

"Come on, Grey." Maria patted him on the arm and started leading him toward the living room. "Let's go get you set up on the couch until it's time to go." She turned as they left and gave Cora a proud smile.

Relief flooded her system as the adrenaline ebbed. Cora let out a deep breath. Only then did she realize Dare was standing beside her.

"For the record?" He paused until he had her full attention. "Who knew having a nurse in the family would come in so handy. It's been great seeing you this weekend, Cora. I sincerely hope it won't be another five years." With that, he winked and went to help Flynn with the rest of the shoveling.

Cora stared after him as his words repeated themselves in her head. Dare still considered her family? She knew Maria often said the same thing. Working this whole friendship thing out with Grey wasn't going to be easy, but for the first time in a long time, Cora didn't feel so alone.

CHAPTER FOURTEEN

A s it turned out, their timing that morning was pretty much spot on. By noon, the roads leading from the cabin into town and the airport were plowed clear. Grey sobered as they left the cabin, but he didn't have time to dwell on it for long. Dare drove them to the first cabin where Grey and Cora retrieved the truck they'd had to leave there Friday night. Once they got to the airport, it was so crowded and hectic that all thoughts of what waited back in Texas flew from Grey's mind.

They checked in at the airport and were told they'd have to wait until their flight information was figured out.

Cora brought Pogo with her. Dare had found some rope to use as a leash, although the dog didn't stray far from Cora. Now that they had internet again, she'd posted on a local online bulletin board and included a picture of Pogo. His happy owners quickly responded and said they'd make it to the airport to pick him up. It turned out that the poor dog had gotten lost shortly after the blizzard began, and the family had feared never seeing him again.

He saw the sadness in Cora's eyes when she patted Pogo

128

before handing him over to an airport employee. On the other side of security, a family with two young children surrounded Pogo with cheers and hugs as the dog's tail wagged happily.

"You did a good thing there," Grey told her.

"I know. I just got attached to the guy. He was the dog I always wanted and never had." She sniffed and then chuckled wryly. "Silly, right?"

"No, it's not silly."

"Well, he's definitely better off with them, though. He'd have to fly in the cargo hold and be locked away in my apartment all the time if he came with me. Assuming I could sneak him past my apartment managers." She laughed, but there was little humor in her eyes. Just sadness and exhaustion. She pointed to his leg. "We'd better find some place for you to sit down."

He wasn't going to argue with her. By the time they returned to where the rest of the family waited, his leg was throbbing.

Flynn and his family were the first to get a flight on a plane to Denver where they'd board a connecting flight to San Antonio. Thankfully, before they left, Flynn had been able to reschedule his interview for the following morning.

The airline was able to fit the rest of them on a separate flight to Dallas/Fort Worth. Mom and Dare would catch a connecting flight to San Antonio from there. Even though they were on the same flight, their seats were so spread out that Grey, sitting on the aisle, could only see Mom a few rows behind him. He knew where Cora was up ahead even though he had no view of her at all. Dare was somewhere on the flight, but Grey hadn't seen which seat he'd been assigned.

The flight felt like an eternity. Even on acetaminophen, Grey's leg was killing him by the time they landed. Trying to get down that narrow aisle without hitting it on anything wasn't easy. Cora waited for him in her row and then disembarked with him. Mom and Grey checked the connections board on the outside of the gate.

Dare glanced at his watch. "It looks like we have about forty minutes before our next flight to San Antonio. That's not much time."

Mom's eyes widened. "We're going to need to find the restrooms and then get something to eat. I'm starving."

"We can wait with you all," Grey told them. He was reluctant to just walk out and leave them there. But the moment the words were out of his mouth, both objected.

"Not with that leg," Mom said firmly. "You go home and get some rest." She hugged him tight with tears in her eyes. Then she turned to Cora. "You, too, honey. Thanks for coming. We've missed you."

Seeing Mom sad was hard enough but watching Cora as she hugged his family and tried to hold back tears was even more difficult. His chest felt tight, and he had to keep himself from reaching for her hand.

They weaved their way through the airport, retrieved their checked luggage, and then took a seat on one of the benches.

Cora regarded his leg. "Are you going to be able to drive home?" Concern knit her brows together.

"I'll be fine since my right leg isn't bothering me," he assured her. Though he had to admit driving all the way home was less than appealing. "All I have to do is get into my car, and the rest will be easy."

She didn't look at all convinced. "Is it okay to ask that you text me when you get home? Just so I know you made it okay?" There were tears in her eyes again, and the fact that they were for him made him both feel bad and hopeful.

"Yes, it's okay. If you promise to do the same for me when you get home."

Cora nodded, then bit her lower lip. She gave a shaky laugh. "We'd better get outside. What lot did you park in?" They had perfect timing and didn't have to wait long for a shuttle.

Mom and Dare were probably boarding the plane by the time they reached the lot where Cora had parked. The shuttle stopped, and the doors opened. The driver wrestled her suitcase from the storage area and waited for her on the pavement.

Cora stood and turned to Grey, her eyes swimming with mixed emotions. "I guess this is it. Don't forget to text me, okay?"

"I won't." He got to his feet and stood with little weight on his left leg. "Come here." He pulled her to him in a hug that didn't last nearly as long as he needed it to. "We're friends again, remember? Which means this isn't goodbye."

She nodded and offered him one more watery smile before stepping off the shuttle.

IT'D BEEN two days since Cora got home from Colorado, and she was still having a difficult time adjusting to her normal work schedule. It didn't seem having three days off would make that much of a difference, but the twelve-hour shifts were brutal.

She did have something else to look forward to. After exchanging texts to let each other know they'd gotten home safely, Cora and Grey had continued to text a couple times a day since. Every time Cora heard her phone chime, the sound never failed to bring a smile to her face.

While texting was great, it was weird not hearing his voice or seeing his smile. She knew the decision to remain friends made a lot of sense, and that only seeing each other occasionally was part of the deal. The problem? She missed him. She was the one who insisted on keeping any relationship they had firmly in the friend zone, which meant she couldn't blur that line, no matter how much she missed him.

Cora yawned as the ER clock struck two in the morning. Hopefully she'd get used to the weird hours again in another day or two.

Jen passed her a cup of coffee. "Don't worry, I made it this time."

"Thank you." Cora took a long drink and willed the caffeine to kick in.

"You still not sleeping?"

"Well, not when I'm supposed to." Cora groaned. "That trip seriously messed me up."

"In more ways than one." Jen raised an eyebrow at her in a knowing way.

She'd somehow managed to wrangle most of the events out of Cora. The only thing Cora didn't reveal was how she and Grey had shared an amazing kiss that still had Cora weak in the knees when she thought about it.

It was enough, though. Jen insisted Cora was still in love with her ex, and while Cora verbally denied that, she knew Jen was right. All the more reason to keep their friendship limited to texts and the occasional passing-by in person.

One of their coworkers tapped the desk on the way by. "Patient coming in. Room three."

Cora set her coffee cup down. "That's me. Alright, I'll see you in a bit. Don't have too much fun, now."

Jen laughed. "I'll try to control myself."

Cora was still smiling when she picked up the clipboard at the nurse's station and scanned the information. Grey's name jumped right out at her. Her eyes moved to the symptoms and saw he was complaining of redness around a wound and a fever.

Her stomach dropped as she realized his cut had become infected. She'd wondered when they might run into each other again but hadn't pictured this particular scenario. The moment she walked through the door in room three, her heart rate kicked up a notch. "Hi."

"Hi yourself." Grey smiled, but it didn't quite reach his eyes. He clearly didn't feel well.

There was probably an ER closer to where he lived. Wouldn't it have been easier if he'd gone there instead? She tried not to overthink his reasons for driving all the way out here.

"When did you start feeling bad? You never mentioned it."

"There was nothing to mention. I thought everything was fine until I felt tired this afternoon. I went home and fell asleep. When I woke up, my leg was hurting." He carefully lifted the leg of his sweatpants. "I thought I'd better take a look and found this." He started to unwrap the bandage, but Cora took over for him.

She lifted the gauze and cringed at the red, angry skin all along the cut. "Yeah, you've definitely got an infection here." She put the gauze back on. "We're going to clean this up, but first I'm going to get your vitals and we'll go from there." It was all business as usual until she looked up and met his eyes. Why did her heart have to stutter like this every time?

"Sounds good."

Cora recorded his blood pressure, pulse, temperature, and checked his oxygen absorption level. He had a low-grade fever, and his blood pressure and pulse were both high, all normal responses to an infection.

Doctor Coalson walked in then and shook Grey's hand. "Alright, let's see what we have here."

Fifteen minutes later, he'd instructed Cora in what he wanted done and told Grey he'd be back after the results were in.

Cora made some notes in Grey's file and then turned to him with a smile. "I'm going to get an IV placed, take some blood so we can check your white blood cell count, and then we'll get you some fluids. Depending on what the blood results are, we may give you some antibiotics through the IV to give your body a chance to start feeling better."

"That works."

She got her supplies together and rolled a chair up to his left side. She got the tourniquet in place and gently felt his arm for the vein she wanted. "There we go." She began to disinfect the area. "Did you ever go see a doctor after you got back?"

"I really don't think this is the time for me to answer that question. Not with that needle in your hand."

Cora shook her head as a smile tugged at her lips. With one fluid motion, she got the catheter in and proceeded to tape it in place. She filled vials with the blood the lab needed before she spoke again. "There. Now, about that answer…"

"My leg was sore, but I felt fine. I'd scheduled an appointment with my doctor for Tuesday to have the stitches removed and figured that would be fine. Obviously, I should've gone in sooner." He looked annoyed with himself. "I was going to wait and go in to see my doctor tomorrow, but the fever had me worried."

"You were right to come in tonight instead. You don't want to mess with infections like this." She finished labeling the vials of blood and got to work hanging some saline solution and getting it dripping into his IV. "If it makes you feel any better, infection is very rare. Sometimes you just can't control how the die rolls."

"I appreciate that. You know me, I don't like screwing up." There was sincerity in his voice.

Cora resisted the urge to reach out and touch his hand. "I know." She lifted the vials of blood. "I'm going to get these to the lab for you, then I'll be back with some medication to help with the pain."

"Thanks, Cora."

"No problem." She gave him a comforting smile before stepping out of the room. Only then could she draw in a deep breath and try to calm her racing thoughts. She'd just started getting used to the idea of only keeping in touch through text and now Grey was here in her ER. Was this random, or was God trying to tell her something?

She distracted herself by taking the blood to the lab. Jen caught her in the hall on the way back.

"Hey, what's going on? You look like you've seen a ghost."

Cora momentarily considered not telling her but knew that wasn't going to do any good. "You know Grey, the ex I just spent the weekend with?"

"Do you have more than one?"

"No. He's the guy in room three."

Jen's jaw dropped before she looked entirely too pleased. "You're kidding me. What did you do? Did he say anything to you?"

"I took his blood like a vampire and then asked him out on a date."

Jen looked thrilled for half a beat before she realized her friend was kidding. "That's not funny."

"Neither is why he's here, Jen. Keep a lid on the enthusiasm, okay? He's here because he has an infected cut on his leg—"

"—that you heroically stitched up in a blizzard—" Jen placed her hands on her hips.

"—so I'm just going to do my job and that's that." When Jen started to say something, Cora held up her hand to stop her. "I'm not talking about it anymore."

Jen tried to suppress a smile but did a poor job of it. "You keep telling yourself that, girl. You keep telling yourself that."

GREY TRIED to relax while he waited for Cora. She'd seemed surprised to see him there, although she'd recovered quickly. He wondered if she'd thought about him even half as much as he'd thought about her over the last two days.

When they'd gone their separate ways at the airport, he'd done his best to be content with merely staying in touch through texts. He hadn't wanted to push their renewed friendship too quickly. He'd been trying to decide whether he could get away with calling her or not when this blasted infection started up.

Driving the extra distance to her ER was a no-brainer. She was the one who knew how he'd cut his leg in the first place and had sewn it up on the fly. It made more sense for her to look at it now.

The moment she'd walked into his room, he knew he'd made the right decision. He had every intention of winning his ex-wife back. For now, though, he was thankful that something good was coming out of this new medical development.

When Cora returned ten minutes or so later, she brought

the medication with her. "I'm going to put this into your IV. No sense in putting another hole in your arm." She flashed him a smile. "And hopefully that'll start to kick in soon. The doctor's going to wait for the blood results and then we'll get in there, clean up your leg, and get you on some antibiotics to knock this infection out." She added a few more notes to his online chart. "Do you have any questions?"

He shivered. When people said hospitals were cold, they weren't kidding. Of course, Grey knew his fever probably wasn't helping him any. He wanted to ask her for a blanket but hesitated. "You're really good at this, you know that?"

"I'm just doing my job." She sounded casual, but there was a pleased smile on her face.

"I'm serious, Cora. You definitely found your calling."

"Thank you." She must have noticed the goose bumps on his arms. "Do you want a blanket?"

"That would be great."

"I'll be right back." She returned a few minutes later with a blanket that she carefully spread over him. "There you go. Let me know if you need a second one."

He nodded. The blanket was warm and immediately Grey's eyelids felt heavier.

She started to leave again but paused and came back. With a glance to the door, she lowered her voice and asked, "So what brought you to this ER? Just in the neighborhood, or…"

"I'm pleading the fifth on the grounds that I'm in pain and now drugged." He raised an eyebrow at her.

She gave him a "whatever" look, but a little smile graced her lips. "Try to relax for a bit. If you need me, just press this button." She handed him the remote before leaving the room again.

Grey didn't know how long it'd been, just that he'd dozed

off and was awakened when Dr. Coalson returned with a knock on the doorframe. "Well, you've definitely got one stubborn infection going on, but I think we should be able to knock it out with some antibiotics through your IV and then a round of oral antibiotics. We'll get that leg cleaned up and bandaged again, too. Let me take another quick look at your leg, and then I'll leave it up to Nurse Wells to get you all fixed up."

"That'll be great. Thank you, doctor."

"No problem." Dr. Coalson pulled on some gloves and then sat on a chair near Grey's bed. Once he had the bandage off, he touched the skin in several places.

Cora came in and hung another bag for his IV, this one with an antibiotic solution.

Grey flinched when the doctor touched an especially sensitive spot.

"Excellent stitching here."

Grey and Cora exchanged amused looks.

"Alright. Nurse Wells, if you'll irrigate the wound, use some antibiotic cream and then bandage it up again, I think we'll have Mr. Jackson here all set." He then gave some directions on how often to change the bandaging and when to see his doctor. "If you have any further questions, just ask for me. Meanwhile, I hope you get to feeling better."

"I appreciate that. Thank you very much."

Dr. Coalson nodded, removed his gloves and then dropped them in the trash on the way out.

Grey couldn't stop the grin on his face. "Did you hear that? He's a fan of your stitching."

"Hush." She whacked him gently on his shoulder. "I'm going to get what I need to clean…"

She was interrupted when a woman brought in the kit

Cora needed. The newcomer was trying hard to look uninterested and failed miserably.

"You might as well have a pair of binoculars around your neck or an ear to the wall, Jen."

The woman pursed her bottom lip out in a dramatic pout. "I have no idea what you're talking about."

Cora shook her head. "Grey, this is my friend, Jen. Jen, this is Grey."

Grey gave her a wave. "You must be the friend that's always trying to fix her up on dates."

When most people might be embarrassed by that revelation, Jen only smiled proudly. "And you must be the man that's had Cora in a funk since she got home."

Grey didn't miss that Cora not-so-subtly kicked Jen in the leg.

"I'm pretty sure you have your own patients to attend to. Right, Jen?"

"Absolutely. It was nice to meet you, Grey."

"You, too." He waved as she left before turning a grin in Cora's direction. "A funk, huh?"

"Shut up, Grey."

He chuckled as Cora got to work cleaning his leg. She worked quickly, her gentle hands moving expertly, and then bandaged his leg again. "Okay, you've got probably another good forty minutes on that antibiotic. You may as well lay back and relax for a bit." She pointed to the control. "You know what to do if you need anything."

An hour later, his antibiotic had finished, and he was cleared to go home. Cora carefully removed the IV from his arm and pressed gauze against the small wound. He laid his hand down on top of hers. "Thank you, Cora."

She paused for several heartbeats, her gaze colliding with

his, before saying, "You're welcome." She put a bandage on top of the gauze and moved away.

He signed the release papers and carefully got to his feet.

"I really wish you had someone take you home." Cora glanced at the clock. "I'd do it, but my shift isn't over for another three hours."

Her concern warmed his heart. "I'll be fine. I'm going straight home, getting some sleep, and I'll fill the antibiotics after I get some sleep. I'll text you when I get home. Will that make you feel better?"

She nodded. "Just be careful. And promise me you'll go see your doctor if this gets any worse, or if the antibiotics don't start clearing things up in a couple of days."

"I promise."

"Good night, Grey."

"'Night, Cora. Thanks again."

He felt better now than he had before going to the ER. Between the pain medication, fluids, and antibiotics, his leg wasn't throbbing nearly as bad as it had been.

He got home and was about to text Cora when he thought of something better. He took a thumbs-up selfie while standing on the porch of his house. It was dark, but the porch light illuminated him enough. He sent that along with a message saying, "I'm home. Going to go sleep this off for a while."

Grey went into his house, checked on a few things, and then collapsed on his bed. He was just about to drift off when his phone chimed with a text from Cora.

"Good. Feel better soon. I'll check on you tomorrow."

"I'd like that."

Grey prayed that this would be the start of truly reconnecting again with Cora and fell asleep with a smile on his face.

CHAPTER FIFTEEN

G rey went back to work on Saturday. His leg felt much better now that the antibiotics had brought the inflammation down. In fact, where the pain had been annoying before, a constant itch had taken over. He was more than ready for his leg to heal so he could get back to normal again.

One good thing had come out of this infection, though. He and Cora had been talking every day since his trip to the ER.

Most of the time, it was through text. But that day after he got back, she'd called him to see how his leg was doing. Grey took his cue from her and every day since, he'd called her in the evening before she went to work.

Today, he knew she had the day off. Meanwhile, he had a lot of work to do, including a stack of paperwork and several customers who had made appointments for later that afternoon. Brody could handle almost anything that came through the store, but occasionally they had customers who wanted to sell something large or obscure that Grey needed to check out and approve first.

He was sorting through those papers in the back office when Brody ducked in. "Hey, Boss Man. There's a woman up front to see you. Says her name is Cora."

Cora was here? He stood and went around to the front of his desk. "Go ahead and bring her in."

"Sure thing."

Moments later, he returned with Cora in tow. She carried herself with purpose, but there was a hint of uncertainty in her eyes.

"Thanks, Brody."

Brody tipped an imaginary hat and left the office.

Cora took in the office. "Your store is nice. It's got a great feel to it, and it's a lot bigger than I pictured." She took a seat when Grey motioned to it. "You're doing really well for yourself here."

"Thank you." He sat down in his chair again. "We originally bought this place because it was big enough to do what I planned and have some room to grow. It was expensive up front, but it turned out to be a worthwhile investment." He took in the way she was holding her hands in her lap and sitting like a statue. "Is everything okay?"

"I was out doing errands, and I ended up in this area. I knew you were returning to work for the first time today, and I guess I just wanted to check in and see how things were going." Her cheeks turned a pretty shade of pink. "Although now I'm thinking I probably should have done that by text. I can go..."

Not on his life. "No, I'm glad you came by." That she made the effort to come in was more than encouraging.

"Really?" She looked relieved as she relaxed a little. "I nearly talked myself out of it two or three times on my way over." She laughed nervously. "I wasn't sure how far this friendship truce really reached."

"I'm trying to figure it out, too. Besides, I visited where you work. It's only fair that you visit me here." He used his good leg to push his chair away from the desk. "Truthfully? The leg is feeling quite a bit better. It's not so much the walking that bothers me as bumping into things. I had no idea I was this clumsy before."

Cora thought a moment. "It will have been a week tomorrow since you cut your leg. You can have the stitches removed anytime." She shook her head. "It feels like it's been so much longer than a week, doesn't it?"

"Yes, it does." It'd be great to get the stitches removed. That had to help with the itching. "I was planning on going in to see my doctor on Monday. Or is that something you could do and save me a copay?"

She looked surprised at his question. "I could definitely remove them for you. It really depends on what you're comfortable with."

That was an easy decision. "I'd prefer it if you'd do it." He couldn't quite tell what she was thinking, and the last thing he wanted to do was make her uncomfortable. "You know, I don't want to take advantage of your nursing skills, Cora. It's okay, I'll go see my doctor on Monday."

"No, it's fine. I really don't mind." It looked like there was something else she wanted to say, but she held back. "You'll have to text me your address, I'm afraid the selfie from that night after you left the hospital isn't much to go on."

He laughed. "Not a problem." He went ahead and sent the address while he was thinking about it. "Is tonight okay?"

"Sure, that'll be fine. What time are you off work?"

"Let's go with five-thirty." He paused. "Is there any chance I could get you to stay for dinner? Nothing fancy, just something to say thanks." He half expected her to decline

143

immediately and was surprised when she only thought a moment before answering.

"Dinner sounds good."

They smiled at each other in an awkward yet understanding way. It reminded Grey of when they were back in high school. They were interested in each other then, yet both afraid to say anything.

Cora stood from her chair. "Well, I should go and let you get back to work." She pointed to the large stack of papers on his desk.

He groaned. "Yeah, things built up when I was gone. I hate paperwork. I'll see you later?"

"I'll be there." With a little wave, she turned and walked out of his office.

Hurting his leg had been unfortunate, but he was thankful it'd happened. If it weren't for that injury, he doubted he and Cora would be talking right now. Satisfied with how things were progressing between them, he tried to switch gears and focus on getting some work done.

THAT EVENING, Grey made sure his house was picked up and at least the bathroom had been cleaned. He'd thought about what he should make for dinner and finally settled on ordering pizza. He wanted to wait and make sure she still liked the same kind of pizza first, though.

Cora arrived right on time. He opened the door and ushered her inside. "Did you find the place okay?"

"I did." She took in the living room. "This is really nice. Do you own it?"

"I just rent. Although I've been impressed enough with

the neighborhood that I'd consider it if the owners ever think about selling." He took the heavy jacket she was wearing and laid it over the top of a small table nearby. "It looks like fall may be finally settling in, doesn't it?"

"It's about time, too." She smiled. "Can you believe Thanksgiving is less than two weeks away? It'll be Christmas before we know it."

The year did seem to be flying by. "So, I figured we'd just order pizza since cooking has never been my strong point."

"Your spaghetti was always good."

He grinned. "That all came from jars, and I think time has clouded your memory of how truly terrible it was." They both laughed. "Is Italian sausage still your favorite?"

"Yes, but with black olives included."

He nodded as he made a mental note. "Interesting combination. Okay, let me call that in. Then maybe we can get the stitches out before it gets here."

"That sounds like a plan."

He called and placed the order. Meanwhile, Cora rummaged through her medical kit and pulled out a small pair of scissors.

"This should be easy. I'm just going to wash my hands and pour some alcohol over these scissors and we'll be ready to go."

She didn't wear gloves this time, and her soft, warm fingers gently tugged on the stitches after she cut them. She pointed to the tiny holes in his skin that they left behind. "These should close up, and you'll barely be able to see them. With this kind of injury, the stitches needed to stay in longer to heal properly, which always increases the chance they'll leave behind scars as well." She told him about a cream he could get and apply that would minimize the scarring.

145

He thanked her, although he wasn't too concerned about how obvious the scar was since it was just on his leg.

"Thank you. That already feels a lot better. They were getting itchy."

"I'm sure." She cleaned up her supplies and set the medical bag on the table by her jacket. "Have you talked to your mom at all since the trip? How is she doing?"

"She's good. Already talking about what she's cooking for Thanksgiving this year."

"Oh, your mom's Thanksgiving meals were always the best. I order those turkey meals from Boston Market now. They are really good, but still don't hold a candle to your mom's cooking."

Mom would appreciate knowing that. Although the thought of Cora eating Thanksgiving dinner alone bothered him. "Oh! Flynn got that job he interviewed for."

Cora smiled. "That's great! I'm sure that's a huge relief for all of them. Any news on Dare? Did his boss forgive him for not being at work on Monday?"

"He's still got his job, but poor Dare isn't sure he'll get Thanksgiving off. I guess his boss was pretty upset he wasn't there despite the fact Dare had a good reason. I told him he should look for another job after the new year."

"That's messed up. He really should. But it'd be good for him to stick it out until then." Her mouth lifted in a smile. "You were quite the hit with Jen. She didn't stop talking about you for the rest of that shift. I thought about setting the two of you up."

Grey didn't expect that and sat, unsure of what to say.

That's when she laughed. "I'm kidding. About the setting you guys up part. I don't think she'd be your type."

She was right. He only had one type, and Cora fell right

into the description of the perfect woman for him. "And what makes you say that?"

"Because she has a strict rule about not dating the same guy for more than three weeks before breaking it off. She thinks the solution to all of the relationship issues out there is to not have one."

"Wow. That's incredibly sad and jaded."

"Yep." It was clear she'd obviously accepted Jen for who she was.

"And you two are friends because…"

"We balance each other out, I guess." Cora shrugged. "I'm trying to convince her to see things differently. And she keeps me from spending all of my free time reading books in my apartment."

That took him back to when they were in school, and it concerned him. "You're doing okay, right?" She gave him a funny look, so he elaborated. "I mean, you're happy. Content with your life."

Her eyes narrowed a little. "Where is that question coming from?"

"I just remember how you'd hide out in your room when school or your parents got overwhelming. I just wanted to make sure it wasn't a defense mechanism for you now."

"A lot has changed, Grey. Just because I'm reading in my apartment instead of bar hopping doesn't mean I'm unhappy." There was an irritated tone to her voice.

"That's not what I meant…"

Someone rang the doorbell. Cora jumped to her feet as though eager to end their conversation. "I'll bet that's the pizza. You want me to chip in?"

"Nah, I've got it." He paid the delivery driver, tipped him, and set the two boxes on the kitchen table. "We've got Italian sausage with black olives for the lady, and supreme for me." He pointed to a cabinet. "Plates are up there if you want to grab a couple for us. I'll get the napkins."

They sat down on opposite sides of his little table, their knees not quite touching each other beneath. After Grey said a prayer for the food and for getting them all home safely again after last weekend, they began to eat.

"I didn't mean to offend you with my question earlier." He paused, trying to formulate his thoughts into words. "I guess, after last weekend, I've found it difficult not to think about you. I just wanted to make sure you have a support system in place. We all need that."

Her features softened. "I have a few friends. People that would help me if I asked, and that goes both ways. I'll admit I probably focus more on my work than I should."

"You're doing a lot of good for a lot of people. That's something to be proud of." He meant every word.

"I appreciate that." She picked a piece of sausage off her pizza and popped it into her mouth. "For the record? You may have entered my thoughts a few times since the trip, too."

Grey nodded slowly and hid his smile with another bite.

They ate and talked mostly about the previous weekend. Comparing notes about things that people had said and done was interesting since they didn't have a whole lot of time to talk openly about it at the cabin.

Once they'd finished their pizza, Grey stood again. "Do you have room for dessert?"

She gave him a look as though she couldn't believe the question. "Of course!"

He closed the boxes of pizza before putting them in the fridge. Then he got two bowls out of the cabinet and retrieved the carton of mint chocolate chip ice cream he'd purchased earlier that day. When he held it up for Cora to see, her face brightened, just like he'd hoped it would.

"You remembered."

Remembered that this was her favorite ice cream? He'd never forgotten. Over the years, he'd alternated between avoiding it because it reminded him of her, and eating some to relive those good memories. He didn't tell her any of that, though. Grey simply smiled and scooped some ice cream into both bowls before storing the carton in the freezer again. After placing a spoon in each, he handed a bowl to Cora.

"Thank you." She took a bite and nodded her approval. "So good." Then she laughed. "Do you remember that time we finished the ice cream at your house, and Dare got so mad at us?"

Grey grinned. "He was furious. An hour or two after you went home, the ice cream truck came through the neighborhood, and Dare hounded me until I went out and bought him something. I've never seen someone love sweets like that guy."

Cora shook her head, a wide smile on her face. "Okay, did you know he's quite the matchmaker?"

His eyes widened. "How's that?" He knew Dare had spoken to him at length but had no idea his brother had done the same with Cora. Grey took a bite of his own ice cream.

"Oh, he was somewhat subtle, but he pretty much insinuated that you and I were a good team, and that he hoped he'd be seeing me again soon."

She was still chuckling, and he joined her, but he really wanted to know what she thought about that. He happened to agree with Dare, but did Cora? "I don't think he's wrong."

"True. We can be a pretty hard team to beat."

"When we stopped working together and watching each other's back is where we messed up."

They looked at one another, and Grey was pretty sure the echo of memories in her eyes reflected the same in his. At some point, they lost that connection somehow, and they'd both suffered for it.

The question of the night was whether it was too late for them to find their way back again.

CHAPTER SIXTEEN

Cora loved how easy it was to fall back into a rhythm of talking and laughing with Grey. But then there were moments where she felt like they were dancing around a subject without quite hitting on it completely.

Grey was right, though. When they worked together and were always there for each other, they were an impossible team to beat. There was no doubt in Cora's mind that, when things were good, they were stronger together than she was on her own.

"I know there are a lot of things that went wrong in our marriage," she began as she picked at one corner of her thumbnail. "I always felt, though, that if I hadn't insisted you go on that trip things might have gone differently."

"I shouldn't have left. You were so detached, Cora, and it killed me to not be able to help you. You didn't seem to need me. I didn't want to go on that trip. I wanted to stay with you, talk about the baby, figure things out." He shrugged. "When I said I'd stay, I was hoping you'd ask me to. You pushed me away again, and I guess that was just all I could take."

His words caused Cora's heart to break all over again.

Tears came to her eyes, and Grey immediately reached for her hand.

"Please don't be upset. I'm not telling you this to make you feel bad. I guess I'm trying to be honest about how I felt that night. Something I should've done a long time ago."

She sniffed. "I know." She got a napkin and dabbed at her eyes. "I know I wasn't easy to be around. I was hurting and yet determined to act as though everything was fine. Thinking about it was bad enough. I guess I figured talking about it would be even worse." She swallowed hard. Saying all of this now was incredibly difficult, but he was right. This was all stuff they should've said years ago. "When you came to me about that trip, I thought it was your way of escaping. Everything was a nightmare then, so I didn't blame you. Telling you to go was one of the hardest things I'd ever done." Cora shrugged, afraid to voice her next thought. "There was a big part of me that wanted you to refuse and stay home with me, but you didn't."

Grey blew out a lungful of air and ran the fingers of both hands through his hair. "I had no idea, Cora."

"I know. You couldn't."

"Just like you couldn't have known I'd wanted you to ask me to stay." He stared at the clock on the wall as though each tick of the second hand represented the moments that the two of them had let slip through their fingers.

Cora's stomach hurt, and she abandoned the rest of her ice cream. She folded her arms over her middle and inhaled slowly to clear her mind a little. She'd wanted Grey to stay that night, and so did he. Neither of them had been able to tell the other. That inability to communicate was the biggest factor in their failed marriage.

Grey stood, moved his dining chair next to hers, and then sat down again. He slid an arm around her shoulders and drew her into a one-arm hug. "Good." He pressed a kiss to the top of her head. "Look, I know that you're not there yet. But in the interest of being open and honest, you should know that I want to try all of this again. The friendship, relationship, marriage. All of it. Because I think the mistakes we made could've been avoided, and we know better now." He gently tipped her chin up until her gaze met his. "I love you, Cora. Is there any chance you could learn to love me again, too?"

His lips touched hers in a brief kiss that was as sweet and gentle as it was healing. Their contact melted her heart. Cora wished the fear of repeating the past would disappear as easily.

When they parted, she touched his chin with her thumb before dropping her hand. "I've always loved you, Grey. I still do." Her voice shook.

He looked into her eyes, his own shining with a mixture of love, determination, and a hint of disappointment. "But?"

"I don't want to mess us up again. I'm not sure we can go back to where we were. And honestly, I'm not sure I want to, either. Not after how it ended." She searched for the right words. "I think we need to go forward as the people we are now and get to know each other that way."

She prayed he'd understand. Her heart fell to the floor when he stood from the chair and turned away from her.

A moment later, he faced her again with a charming smile on his face. "In that case, Cora Wells, will you go steady with me?" He winked at her.

Cora giggled as relief flooded her system. "I'd like that." But a moment later, she sobered again. "Promise you'll tell me the important stuff, even if you're afraid I'll be angry or that my feelings will be hurt. I..." her voice clogged with emotion, and she shook her head.

"I'll promise that, if you'll do the same for me." He reached for her hand again and held it tightly in his. "No matter what it is. The way I figure it, if we can sit here and have this conversation after everything that's happened between us, we can handle anything. Especially if we do it together."

His words slid over old wounds like salve on a burn that had been festering for far too long. "I promise."

They talked about some of the things they could do together as they cleaned up after dinner. Cora looked at the clock and was surprised to see it was so late. "I should probably head home, Grey." She wished she didn't have to.

He smiled at her. "Thank you again for your help with the stitches. I appreciate it."

"Not a problem. Thank you for the pizza. I must admit the evenings get a little long sometimes, so it was nice to get out for a while. I had fun, Grey."

His smile widened. "So did I. If you're comfortable with it, could you send me your work schedule? The next time we both have the day off, we'll have to go do something fun for the day."

"I'd like that." The thought of having things like this evening to look forward to had Cora feeling lighter than air. She retrieved her jacket and bag.

He went into the kitchen and came back with a pizza box. "You should take this, too. It'll make a great midnight snack. I'll walk you out."

After flipping the porch light on, they walked out to her car together. She set the pizza and her bag on the passenger seat first before going around to the driver's side. Grey opened the door for her. She started to get in and then turned back to say something else. The words fled her mind, though, when he was standing right behind her, one hand on the door and the other on the roof of her car.

Their amazing, toe-curling kiss at the cabin replayed itself in her mind. Her heart begged for her to lean in for a repeat while her brain told her it was time to go before she did something stupid. She wasn't sure she could start kissing him and ever stop. As she was still trying to decide which impulse was going to win out, Grey made the decision for her.

He pressed a lingering kiss to her cheek. "Be careful driving home. Will you let me know when you get there?"

"Of course." She gave him a final smile before getting in. He shut the door for her. As she pulled away from the curb, she noticed he stood in front of his house until she was out of sight.

He'd been the perfect gentleman. Part of her was disappointed that he didn't truly kiss her goodbye, but a bigger part of her appreciated the fact that he was taking her concerns seriously. She sensed he was letting her set the pace in this newfound relationship of theirs.

The truth was, she knew what she wanted. She was just afraid that saying it aloud would mean it'd be that much harder if things fell apart again between them.

Once she'd gone inside and locked the door behind her, she took her phone out and texted Grey. "Okay, I'm home."

His reply came moments later. "Good. Call me if you need anything, okay?"

Her thumbs flew over the keyboard as she typed out her response. "Will do. I had fun tonight. I've missed you, Grey." She hit send and then hoped she wasn't being too emotional. But his response had her smiling again as she read it.

"I know what you mean. I've missed you, too."

❄️

OVER THE NEXT FEW DAYS, Cora spoke to Grey daily on the phone, and sometimes their conversations stretched for two or more hours. Cora got to where she not only enjoyed their conversations but looked forward to them all day.

On Tuesday afternoon, Cora's phone rang. Just hearing the sound made her smile. This time, the number showed it was Maria calling. "Hello?"

"Hi, Cora. It's Maria. How are you doing this afternoon?"

Hearing her voice made Cora smile. "Hi! I'm doing well. How about you?"

"I'm doing wonderfully. I know I'm not giving you a lot of notice, but this month has just gotten away from me. I wanted to call because I'm hosting the family at my house for Thanksgiving this year, and I'd love it if you joined us."

That was the last thing Cora expected to hear. Had Grey told Maria about their renewed relationship, or was this all Maria? If Cora did go, would she and Grey pretend they hadn't started seeing each other again? What would Flynn say if he found out? All of the unknowns had her head swimming and nerves balling in her stomach. There was no way she could give an answer without talking to Grey first.

"I'm not sure about my schedule yet." Which was true. She didn't normally pay much attention beyond the current week because she rarely asked for extra time off. And Thanksgiving? She'd planned on buying a meal from Boston Market and eating it in front of the television.

"I completely understand. I know it's a long way to come for a meal, too. But we thought that, if you drove in with Grey... Anyway, I want you to know that you're welcome here. I have the food covered, so there's no need to bring anything." There was some noise in the background. "I'd better run. Think about it, Cora. I hope you'll join us."

"Thank you for the invitation, Maria, I appreciate it. I'll let you know."

"Sounds good. Bye, honey."

"Bye." Cora ended the call and sat staring at her phone. Her first instinct was to say no, that going to Maria's house for Thanksgiving and having to see Flynn again would be anything but easy. Moments later, though, the thought of spending the holiday with Grey, Maria, and Dare had her smiling. She truly had no idea what she should do and decided she'd check with Grey first.

Later that evening, Cora got out of her car and headed for the hospital. She pulled her jacket closer to ward away the cold. It was only just before eight, but they were expecting a freeze tonight, the first of the season. Since it was already midway through November, they'd gotten away with warmer-than-normal weather for a while and couldn't really complain.

At least she wouldn't be working all night. Cora was covering for Jen until midnight when she'd come in and take her shift over again.

It turned out to be an insanely busy night where one new case arrived after another. By the time Jen came in, Cora was exhausted and ready to be home. They had a lull, though, so Cora told her about Maria's phone call.

"Are you kidding? It's a no-brainer." Jen was staring at Cora as though she'd grown a third eye right in the middle of her forehead. "Go spend Thanksgiving with Grey. What's holding you back?"

Cora blinked at her. "Seriously? Remember the whole tale about Flynn and how he reacted at the cabin?"

"I doubt Maria would've invited you if Flynn was so against it. Maybe he's trying to bury the hatchet." Jen raised an eyebrow. "What else do you have?"

"Let me see…" She dragged it out as though she really had to think about her answer. "Grey and I got divorced. Falling for him again is bad enough, but to go into enemy territory when everything is still new..."

"Oooh! You're falling for him. I *knew* it!"

Cora motioned for her to keep it down. The last thing she needed was for the entire ER to gossip about her love life. "I don't understand how someone who is so adamant against any kind of relationship has the audacity to encourage me to jump back into one that I've already proved didn't work."

"Five years is a long time, Cora. I'm willing to bet you've both changed a lot."

Jen had her there. That was the whole reason behind taking things slow and getting to know each other again.

"The way I see it," Jen continued, "if you don't take a chance, you're going to wonder what would've happened. Thanksgiving is either going to be amazing and you'll be glad you went, or it'll be horrible and put a nail in the coffin of your relationship. Either way, you'll probably have an answer you're looking for. Isn't that worth going for on its own?"

Cora really didn't want to admit that Jen was right, but her expression must have given it away. Jen grinned as though she'd just won the lottery. "That's what I'm talking about. I expect updates from you regularly, girl. I'm serious about that."

"Maybe one of these days I can convince you to give rela-tionships a shot."

Jen raised an eyebrow. "Don't hold your breath."

Cora shook her head at her friend. "You are a mess. Alright, I'm out of here. I hope the rest of your shift goes smoothly."

"Thanks again for covering for me. I owe you one."

"And don't you forget it." Cora gave her a hug and

headed for the front of the ER. It'd gotten colder, and Cora wished she brought her heavier coat. If it wasn't freezing yet, it was close. As she walked across the parking lot to her car, she stopped short. Where was it?

She parked in the same spot, or one close by, every single time. She turned slowly, wondering if she was just too tired to remember parking it somewhere else.

Nothing.

She walked to her usual spot. There was broken glass on the ground. Furious and tired, she jogged back to the hospital and spoke to Ray, the security officer on duty up front. "Hey, I think someone stole my car out of the parking lot."

"Are you sure?"

"Well, either that or someone decided to move it as a prank. At this time of the night, that should be a crime, too."

Ray nodded. "Give me a minute to call it in. We have cameras out there we can check."

Cora paced back and forth before the front desk as Ray called the nearest precinct, relayed the car model, year, and color. When the police arrived, they got her statement, took pictures of the glass on the ground, and confiscated the recorded tape from the time she got to the hospital until she'd discovered her car missing.

One of the officers assured her that they'd do everything they could to find the car. "We're going to go through this tape, and we've got an alert out on your car. We'll call you when we learn anything. Meanwhile, you should be able to contact your insurance in the morning and get a rental."

"Thank you, I appreciate it."

"You're welcome, ma'am. You have someone you can call to take you home?"

Cora nodded even as her mind raced. Her first instinct was to call Grey, but it was almost four in the morning, and she hated to wake him. She could hang out and wait until eight when Jen was off shift and ask her for a ride. Cora really didn't feel like hanging out in the waiting room for that long, though.

She finally cringed and dialed Grey's number.

CHAPTER SEVENTEEN

G rey stayed up way too late watching episodes of one of his favorite television shows before finally going to bed. It took hearing his phone ring for a second time before he sat up in bed and realized it really wasn't part of his dream. With bleary eyes, he looked at the caller ID. The moment he saw Cora's name, he was instantly awake. "Hey. You okay?"

There was a moment of silence. He looked at the screen to see if they'd been disconnected. "Cora?"

"I'm so sorry to wake you up, Grey. Someone stole my car while I was covering a shift at the hospital." She hesitated. "Is there any way you could come and take me home? I'm kinda stuck here."

There was no missing the weariness in her voice. He was already out of bed and reaching for a shirt from his dresser drawer. "Absolutely. You can wait inside, right?"

"Yes."

Good. That made him feel a lot better. "I'll be there as soon as I can."

"Thank you, Grey."

She hung up then. He rushed to get dressed, grabbed his car keys, and began the drive to the hospital. As he drove up to the ER doors, Cora emerged with a tired wave. He reached across the cab of his car to open the door for her.

"I hate that this happened to you," he said as she buckled her seat belt. "Do they have any leads?"

She shook her head. "Just some broken glass on the pavement. There are cameras in the parking lot, but the lighting isn't great in that area, so I'm not sure how much they can see. Of course, they have an alert out on it. Even if they locate it, it'll probably be stripped or wrecked." She released a heavy sigh and rested her arm against the window before leaning her head on it. "I guess I'll call my insurance in the morning. I'll be able to get a rental, but really didn't need to mess with this."

"Of course not." He cleared his throat. "I don't think you ever told me your address."

She glanced at him, a smile lifting the frown from her face. "I suppose I hadn't."

After she told him, he put the car in drive. They both remained silent as he maneuvered his way through the streets of Denton to her apartment complex. It wasn't the nicest he'd seen around town. He stopped at the entrance and softly touched Cora's shoulder. She'd been so quiet, he thought she might've fallen asleep.

She lifted her head and blinked. "Oh. I'm in building seven. It's up ahead on the right." She yawned as she leaned her head against the seat behind her.

With her direction, he found a parking spot, got out, and went around to open her door. "Come on, I'll walk you in." He offered a hand to help her out. When she didn't withdraw hers after she was out of the car, he happily continued to hold it. She led the way to a door on the first floor, unlocked it, and stepped inside.

Grey followed, taking in the small space. From the entry, he could see the kitchen, tiny living room, and a door that led to what looked like a single bedroom. It couldn't be more than six hundred square feet.

He put a hand against her back and directed her to the futon in the living room. "Why don't you sit down and let me get you some water. Where are your glasses?"

"In the cabinet to the right of the sink."

He waited long enough to see she took his advice before heading to the kitchen. When he returned, she took a long drink and sat the glass on the coffee table. "Thank you. Ugh, what a night."

Grey took a seat on the other end of the futon. "I hope they consider putting more lighting in the parking lot."

"To my knowledge, this hasn't happened before. It was probably a fluke and certainly no fault of the hospital." She shrugged, a defeated look on her face. "At least I don't have a shift until eight tonight, so I should be able to get a rental before then. They can bring them to you, right?"

"Yes, they'll bring one to you. But if they don't for some reason, let me know, and I'll drive you to the office to pick it up."

She nodded. "I appreciate it. I'm really sorry for dragging you out at this hour." She yawned again.

"Don't be sorry, Cora. I don't mind helping out." That's why he'd told her to call him if she ever needed him. "Why don't you lie down here and try to get some sleep. I'll get a blanket from your room."

She nodded again and shifted to lie on her side. While she got comfortable, Grey retrieved the comforter from her bed.

By the time he got back in the living room again, her eyes were half closed, and her hands clasped beneath her chin. His heart turned over in his chest as he spread the blanket over her.

He crouched in front of her. "You going to be okay?"

"Yeah. I'll sleep for a while and then call the insurance company when I wake up. Nothing I can do about it all right now anyway." She pointed to her cell phone on the coffee table nearby. "The police will call if they have any news."

He really didn't want to leave her, but he couldn't just sit in the nearby recliner and watch her sleep like a stalker, either. "Sounds like a plan." He started to stand and stopped himself. "Hey, Cora? Thanks for calling me."

Her long lashes lifted, and her hazel eyes focused on him. "You were the first person I thought of." Then they fell again as she drifted off to sleep.

Grey's heart felt as though it might explode. He gently brushed some hair away and pressed a gentle kiss to her forehead. She didn't move a muscle.

"Sleep well, sweetheart."

With that, he locked the door behind him and headed home. He probably should try to get another hour of sleep in, but there was no way this adrenaline rush was going to allow that.

"Thank you for keeping her safe tonight," he prayed aloud as he pulled into his driveway. He didn't get out of his car but simply stared at the side of the house illuminated by the headlights. He drank in the realization that truly mending their relationship seemed like a true possibility.

WHEN CORA WOKE up later that morning, it took her a moment to process why she was sleeping on the couch in the living room. She remembered the situation with her car and how Grey had come to her rescue. She barely remembered him tucking her in under a blanket before falling asleep. He'd been there for her when he didn't have to be. He'd been her hero, just like he used to be.

Cora's heart sped up with that realization. She needed Grey, which was both exciting and scary. She told him they ought to go slow, get to know each other again. All of that made sense. She was afraid to risk her heart but knew full well it was already too late.

Two hours later, she'd taken a shower, talked to her insurance company, and signed for a rental car that was delivered to her apartment. She still hadn't heard from the police, but at least she'd be able to get to work without a problem.

She was starting to think about lunch when her phone rang. When she saw Grey's name, she couldn't stop her smile. "Good afternoon."

"Right back at ya. How are you doing? Any news?"

"Nothing from the police. But I've got a rental car, and they even delivered. Talk about service." She sat down on the futon.

"That's great. Hopefully you'll hear about your car soon." He spoke to someone in the background. "I'm here at a sandwich shop. I'd like to bring you some lunch if you're up to it."

She hadn't thought she'd be seeing Grey again today and was happy to have the opportunity. "That would be awesome. Turkey, swiss cheese, mayo please."

"You got it. I'll be by in the next twenty minutes."

They said goodbye. True to his word, there was a knock on her door not long after. She ushered him in and breathed in the amazing smell of hot sandwiches. "Aren't you working today?"

"I took a long lunch. I'll have to go back in about an hour."

"Well, you are a life saver, Grey. Thank you."

He looked pleased. "You are more than welcome."

They put food on plates and chose to eat in the living room and use the coffee table.

Grey took a bite of his sandwich and nodded appreciatively. "Yep, that hits the spot. So, about your car, did you have anything in it?"

"A book of CDs, but that was it. It's not like the stereo was anything to write home about." She couldn't imagine why someone would want to steal her beat-up car.

"They probably either did it on a dare, or for parts."

"I'm trying to think positively. Maybe this is what I needed to finally get a new car, not that I'm looking forward to payments." She cringed. She'd chosen the car she had now a few years ago with the express purpose of paying cash and not having to leach money from her paycheck every month. She supposed it was bound to happen eventually. "Guess who I heard from yesterday?"

His brows rose. "Who?"

"Your mom. She called to invite me to Thanksgiving dinner." She expected him to be shocked, but he only looked mildly surprised. "Why don't you seem surprised?"

"Because Mom mentioned she was going to and wanted to make sure I was okay with it. I told her I was."

She looked at him curiously. "Then you want me to go?"

"Yep."

His simple, clear answer brought a chuckle out of her. "You don't need to think about it first?"

"Nope." He grinned. "In case I haven't been clear about it, I enjoy spending time with you, Cora. The more of it, the better."

"I'll have to see if I can get a hotel reservation."

"I'm sure Mom would happily let you stay with her." He was watching her with an amused smile on his face. "I know things are still up in the air with your car. You can drive down with me, so you can't use that as an excuse." Now he was just looking downright smug.

Cora balled up her napkin and threw it at him. "Well now, you've just thought of everything." The idea of seeing Flynn and Abby again made her nervous. "I'll talk to my boss. I'm off work for Thursday and Friday, but I'm usually on call. I'll see what I can do."

"Great!"

Cora's phone rang then, and she answered. It was the police officer assigned to her case. After listening to the news, she ended the call with a heavy sigh.

"Any word?"

"Yeah, they found my car. It's been stripped right down to the tires. I guess I'll update my insurance and then wait to see what they're able to do."

"I'm sorry, Cora."

"Thanks. Me, too." She shrugged. "It is what it is. Besides, it's kind of hard to feel too bad about all of the weird things that have been happening lately."

Grey finished his sandwich and set his plate on the coffee table. "What do you mean?"

"The blizzard and getting snowed in, your leg getting infected, my car. It's all resulted in stretching out reasons for the two of us to be around each other." She paused. "I guess what I'm saying is that, while some of those situations were difficult to go through initially, I'm not sorry they happened." She realized how that sounded and her face grew warm. "You know what I mean."

He laughed. "Yes, I know what you mean. And I feel the same way."

They talked for another twenty minutes before Grey said he needed to get back to work. Cora walked him to the door. "Thanks for bringing lunch, Grey, and for bringing me home. You went above and beyond."

"I'm just glad you're okay, and that you were able to get a car quickly so you aren't stranded. But if you do need anything, don't hesitate to call me."

She took her cue from him, raised up on her tip-toes, and pressed a kiss to his cheek. "I'll do that."

CHAPTER EIGHTEEN

The first two days of Thanksgiving week dragged for Grey. Now that it was Wednesday, suddenly all of the things he needed to accomplish seemed to have grown. It'd take a lot to get it all done before closing the store Thursday and Friday for Thanksgiving. He was still working through his to-do list when he got a text from Cora.

"I hope your day is going better than mine."

That had him on immediate alert. "Uh-oh. What's up?"

"I can't go with you to your mom's tomorrow. I'm sorry."

Grey was going to text her back and ask why but decided this was going to be a lot easier with a phone call. He dialed her number and waited several rings for her to pick up.

"Hey."

"I thought we had everything ironed out. Did something change with work?" Her boss had promised her the two days off since she'd worked every holiday for the last couple of years.

"Several nurses, or someone in their family, came down with the flu. Even Jen is laid up at home. I have to work eight in the morning until eight on Thanksgiving night. There's really not much else to be done about it."

He wanted to object, but knew she was right. It was one of the hazards of her job. It was still disappointing, though. "I could stay in town. If you get a lunch break, you could call me."

"No. Grey, you should go spend the holiday with your family. Lunch breaks are usually eaten standing up between patients unless it's a slow day. Trust me, you won't be missing anything here. I'll work this extra shift, and we can see each other this weekend."

Grey didn't like that idea at all. The thought of her spending Thanksgiving by herself bothered him even as he realized that she'd been doing exactly that for the last five years.

"You still there, Grey?"

"Yeah, I'm here. Sorry." He paused. "You sure you want me to go to my mom's?"

"Yes. I'm positive."

"All right." Grey knew that definitive tone to her voice. He didn't want to push her. "I'll text you in the morning?"

"Sounds good. And Grey? I really am sorry."

"I know, Cora. Me, too."

They said their goodbyes. He leaned back in his chair and stared at the calendar on his desk as the multitude of notes blurred together. This was their first holiday since reconnecting. He didn't feel right about leaving her here and driving all the way to San Antonio. At the same time, he knew she hated being pushed into things. If she told him she was fine and wanted him to go...

His mind went to the last time she told him he should leave. He hadn't realized it then, but it'd been a defining moment that led to the end of their marriage. Grey made a mistake then, and he wasn't about to make the same one now.

CORA WOKE up just after seven on Thanksgiving Day with a heavy heart. There'd been absolutely no reason for Grey to stick around town today. He'd be sitting alone at his place, eating TV dinners or something, and she'd feel guilty that she was working instead of keeping him company. Telling him he should go to his mom's house for Thanksgiving was the right decision.

She glanced at her phone to find a text from him.

"Happy Thanksgiving. I miss you already."

Of course he'd have left early to make that drive and have most of the day with his family. She just wished she hadn't slept through his text. She responded, knowing he likely wouldn't see it for a while. "Happy Thanksgiving. I miss you, too. Drive safe, okay?" She hit send before dragging herself out of bed with a groan.

It was going to be a long day. What really stunk was that she was probably too late to reserve a Thanksgiving dinner from Boston Market for tonight. She tried not to think about that as she showered and got dressed for the day.

Her shift at the hospital was long and busy. Between the guy coming in with extensive burns from dropping a turkey into hot oil to the multitudes of holiday car accidents, Cora had little time to sit and rest. Lunch was half of a dry sandwich and a bag of chips, and dinner wasn't much better.

Several times, she thought about texting Grey to let him know she was thinking about him. Every time, she talked herself out of it. He was visiting with his family and enjoying a big Thanksgiving meal about now. The last thing she needed was to make him feel guilty for leaving. It'd been her choice to encourage it, although the selfish part of her now regretted it. She wished she'd agreed to him staying, or at least that he'd stayed anyway despite her assurances to the contrary.

There was no use replaying it over and over in her mind. What was done was done. She just needed to make it through the rest of this shift so she could get home, go to bed, and put this day behind her.

When eight rolled around, Cora was exhausted. At least it wasn't horribly late. She decided to call Grey once she got home to say hello. The thought of talking to him, kicking her shoes off, and finding something besides a stale sandwich to eat for dinner had her feeling a little better.

She parked at the apartment complex. It wasn't until she was a few feet from her front door that she noticed the large vase full of flowers sitting on the step. The yellow, orange, and red daisies brought out a smile as she withdrew the small card and read it.

"Cora, I hope you'll forgive me. Love, Grey."

She read it again as her brows crinkled with confusion. "Forgive him for what?"

Shuffling in the breezeway behind her had Cora whirling around to find Grey standing there with a smile on his face and a large bag in one hand.

"For ignoring your suggestion, not going to San Antonio like we planned, and for staying in town without telling you." He gave her a big smile. "Surprise!"

Cora shook her head slowly, hardly believing that he was standing right there in front of her. "You are something else."

He'd stayed. He'd skipped a huge Thanksgiving dinner, complete with amazing desserts if Maria was still baking like she'd used to. And he'd done it so they could be together. Her heart turned over in her chest.

"A good something or a bad something?"

She chuckled. "It would be a toss-up if it weren't for the flowers." She lifted the vase and then dug around in her pocket for her keys. "They tipped the scale in your favor."

"What if I said I brought dinner with me?"

She got the door unlocked, pushed it open, and motioned for him to go inside. "Now we're talking."

Once they were both inside, she set her bag down and hugged the vase of flowers. "These are truly beautiful, Grey. Thank you so much."

"You're welcome. And I figured you probably hadn't had much to eat at work, and certainly nothing compared to the dinner we were supposed to have. But I was able to procure the next best thing." He held up the bag for her to inspect.

Only then did Cora see the logo. "You didn't. Are you serious?" Her stomach growled just thinking about food from Boston Market.

"I told them I knew a certain nurse who deserved a good dinner on Thanksgiving. Between that and my obvious charms, I managed to talk them out of two meals." Grey's eyes sparkled with humor as he teased her. "I'll get us some plates and silverware if you want to go change, and we'll eat before it gets cold."

"That sounds amazing." Not only had he brought her flowers and dinner, but he remembered something she'd told him in passing a while ago: As soon as she got home from work, she liked to change out of her dirty scrubs and into something cozy and comfortable.

She did just that and returned to find he'd set up the little dining room table complete with a candle he'd placed in the center. The flame danced as the wax around it began to melt.

Cora breathed in the scent of cinnamon and cloves. "Wow, this is amazing."

Grey reached for her hand before closing his eyes. "Dear heavenly Father, we thank You for the chance to spend this holiday together. Please bless this food to the nourishment of our bodies and help us to see how truly fortunate we are."

"Amen." Their words blended together.

He moved to sit down, but Cora snagged his hand to stop him. She stretched up on tip toes, and pressed a kiss to his cheek. She'd intended for it to be a quick peck but lingered a second or two longer. When she drew back and stood normally again, it was clear she had his complete attention. "Thank you for not leaving."

"Thank you for not really wanting me to." He looked into her eyes as though looking for the answer to an unspoken question. He must have found it because he cupped the back of her head with one hand and leaned in to capture her lips with his.

This kiss was different from the hesitant one in Colorado. For Cora, it was full of reminders of what they were together, and of where they could be again. Her heart soared as he thoroughly erased every doubt from her mind.

When he broke their kiss, Cora opened her eyes slowly to find him smiling into her face.

"You are more beautiful now than the day I met you."

His sweet words had her feeling as though she were floating on a cloud.

He played with a section of her hair with his thumb and finger. "I was an idiot, you know."

"Why is that?"

"Because I let you go in the first place."

Cora shook her head. "We were both idiots."

He cradled her face in both of his hands. "I'm so in love with you, Cora."

Her heart felt as though it might burst. "I love you, too."

He kissed her again, and Cora held onto the sleeve of his shirt as he put an arm around her waist to steady her.

A few moments later, he pulled back, a serious look on his face. "I do have one new regret, though."

Her stomach clenched. Was he already second-guessing this change in their relationship? She prayed that wasn't true, because after being reminded how amazing it was to be in his life, she wasn't about to give that up again without a fight. "Oh? What's that?" She took in a deep breath and held it.

"I regret that I didn't swing by the store and get us a pumpkin pie for dessert." His face was still serious except for that twinkle in his eyes.

She smacked him in the chest. "Not funny, Grey."

"Too soon?"

"Oh, yeah." She smiled and happily surrendered to another breathtaking kiss.

CHAPTER NINETEEN

"I can't believe I'm doing this," Cora said with a laugh. Grey had surprised her with a day trip to Gaylord Texan Resort in Grapevine. She'd heard of the place's amazing winter wonderland but had never been there.

After having to work Thanksgiving, her boss had given her a four-day weekend for Christmas. They were driving down to San Antonio Christmas Eve, but Grey insisted they should do something fun before then. He didn't tell her where they were going, simply instructed her to dress warm, bring a coat and mittens, and started to drive.

Now, she stood in line to snow tube down a hill. She was getting close enough to see the packed snow on the lanes in front of them.

Grey put an arm around her and pulled her close so he didn't have to talk too loudly over the crowd. "There were a lot of fun things we should've been able to do in Colorado but missed out on. Sledding was one of them, and this is the next best thing." He grinned at her.

Five minutes later, it was their turn. They sat on their

inner tubes in adjoining lanes. Cora raised an eyebrow and gave him a playful smile. "Race you to the bottom!"

The moment the tube began to slide, cool air whooshed past, tossing her hair. The ride ended much too soon as the tube came to a gentle stop.

Laughing, Cora stood, dusted her pants off, and picked up the inner tube again. "Now *that* was fun."

"Yes, it was." Grey grinned at her. "You want to go down again?"

"Absolutely."

An hour later, with a paper cup of hot chocolate in her hands, Cora settled onto a bench next to Grey. Despite the crowds, they'd managed to find a bench off the beaten path. The extensive ice sculpture display lit up the night while Christmas lights adorned the branches of trees all around them. This particular bench was situated beneath the high boughs of an evergreen. Even with people walking back and forth along the paths, Cora could imagine they were somewhere else entirely.

"Are you warm enough?" Grey looked at her with concern.

His attentiveness made her heart skip a beat. "I'm good, thank you. This was such a great idea, and a wonderful surprise."

"I'm glad you like it." He held his cup of hot chocolate, so far untouched, in one hand and sat silently for a moment. When he shifted, he reached for her cup and set both on the ground to one side of the bench.

Cora turned to face him, confused by his actions and missing the warmth of the cup. The cold air only held her attention for a breath or two until Grey withdrew a small box from the pocket of his coat.

He moved closer to Cora and reached for her hand. Her

breath caught, and tears immediately sprang to her eyes as he began to speak.

"Cora, I've made a whole hill of mistakes over the years. If there's one thing I did right, though, it was falling in love with you. I missed you every day we were apart." He paused. "The day you said you'd marry me, I knew I was the luckiest man alive. If you'd only do the honor of marrying me again, I promise I'll spend the rest of my life showing you just how much you mean to me." He opened the box then and lifted an engagement ring between his thumb and finger. "I love you, Cora. Will you be my wife forever?"

Her heart took flight at his words, and Cora was completely oblivious to the noise of the crowd around them. All that existed was her and Grey and the promise of a second chance that she couldn't deny.

"Yes." A single happy tear escaped from the corner of her eye. "I love you, too."

Grey slipped the ring on her finger. He cupped her cheek with his hand and used his thumb to wipe away the tear. Cora's heart sang as he kissed her then, his arms around her, keeping her warmer than anything else in the world ever could.

IT WAS late morning the day before Christmas, and Grey glanced over at Cora in concern. She'd spent the last half hour of their car ride in silence. From the way she kept spinning her engagement ring around her finger and twiddling with the zipper of her jacket, it was clear she was nervous. Unable to take it any longer, he reached over and took her hand in his.

"It's going to be okay. You need to relax a little."

Cora shot him a look that told him she was far from convinced. "Seeing Flynn and Abby again, especially now that we're engaged, is reason enough to worry. Maybe we should've sent an e-mail to tell people instead of just showing up like this. And we're going to their house. We very well could be walking right into the dragon's den."

He had to stifle a chuckle because he knew she wouldn't appreciate it. Not even if he told her how cute she was right now. "Well, if that's the case, there's a door we can use to make our escape. The most important thing is that we stick together." He held their joined hands up for emphasis.

Cora nodded her agreement and kept mostly silent as he made his way through San Antonio to Flynn and Abby's house. They parked along the curb in front of their two-story colonial-style home. He'd no sooner turned off the engine when Zac came running down the stairs and across the yard.

Cora smiled as she got out of the car and welcomed the boy with a big hug. "Hey, Zac. How are you doing?"

"Good." He held up his thumb with a proud grin. "I has a scar."

Cora held his thumb, her eyes widening appropriately. "Wow, that is one cool scar. Did you see this, Uncle Grey? Check it out."

Grey gave his nephew a fist bump. "Super awesome, buddy." He swung the boy up to sit on his shoulders. "Let's go in and see everyone else. Are Grandma and Uncle Dare here already?"

"Uh-huh." Zac pointed to the house. "In there."

Grey put a hand on Cora's neck and massaged it for a moment. "You ready for this?"

"As ready as I'll ever be."

He took her hand in his and they walked up the steps together. They were met at the door by Abby, who took Zac from Grey's shoulders and set him on the ground. The boy was off and running. "Merry Christmas, you two. I hope your drive was okay."

"Uneventful, which is the way I like it," Grey said as he and then Cora each gave her a hug.

Flynn appeared behind his wife and smiled. Grey could detect a small amount of uncertainty there as he stood to the side so they could enter the house. "I'm glad you could both make it. Welcome." He shook Grey's hand and then, for the very first time, gave Cora a quick hug. "Come on in and make yourselves comfortable."

Mom gave them both a one-armed hug since she was holding Emma in the other.

Grey shook Dare's hand. "Hey, man. I'm glad to see you. Didn't know if you'd get the day off or not."

"You and me both, brother. But when the boss said I could have the day off, I took it and ran before he changed his mind." He chuckled before pulling Cora into a big hug. "Good to see you. Sewn up any cut legs or set any broken bones lately?"

Cora laughed. "Oh, you know, at least once a day." She winked.

Mom smiled as her gaze roamed around the room and touched on each person there. "Look at us. We're all in the same room, no one's fighting, and it didn't even take a blizzard to get us here today."

Dare walked purposefully to the front door, stuck his head out to look around, and closed it again. "Just checking to make sure you didn't just jinx us."

Grey put an arm around Cora's shoulders and pulled her close. "I think we've all had enough snow for a while." He took her left hand in his. "Although I, for one, am thankful we got stuck in that blizzard. It helped us realize that five years is more than long enough to be apart." He held it up so everyone could see the engagement ring on her finger.

Mom squealed as she ran forward to hug them both, tears in her eyes. "Oh, I'm so happy."

It was Dare who said, "Well, it's about time the two of you came to your senses." He and Abby took turns congratulating them.

Grey looked to Flynn, hoping and praying his big brother would be accepting of his decision to marry Cora again.

Flynn gave a nod of approval. "Welcome back, Cora."

EPILOGUE

ONE YEAR LATER

C ora giggled as Grey swooped her into his arms before carrying her across the threshold of the house they'd just closed on. She'd moved into his rental house after they got married ten months ago, but now they had a place of their own. It felt amazing.

"Welcome home." He set her on her feet and then kissed her in a way that was so sweet her heart sighed.

"I'm so glad we're finally here." She smiled up at him, more than content to never step out of his arms again.

He took her hand and led her through the maze of boxes in the living room. They had a lot of work to do to get the house together, but Cora didn't mind.

He stopped in the hallway. "I have one more surprise for you."

Cora blinked at him. "What kind of surprise is it?" She wracked her brain trying to think of what he might have up his sleeve but came up blank.

He led her into the kitchen and pulled a chair out for her. Once she was seated, he instructed her to close her eyes. "Keep them closed until I tell you to open them."

With that, he gave her a brief kiss and moved away from her.

She heard the back door open and close, followed by silence. A few minutes later, it opened again, and she could hear his footsteps on the kitchen floor. There was some shuffling before he finally said, "Okay, Cora. You can open your eyes now."

She did then, and the first thing she saw was Grey's smiling face. Something moved on the floor drawing her attention to their feet. There, staring up at her with hopeful eyes, was a golden retriever puppy. Its little tail wagged back and forth so fast, she wouldn't have been surprised if it wore a spot on the floor.

Cora immediately knelt beside the puppy who didn't hesitate to clamber onto her lap.

Grey sat down on the floor beside them. "He doesn't have a name yet. I thought that, since you've always wanted a dog, you could choose a name for him."

Tears flooded Cora's eyes turning the puppy into a blur of yellow fur. His little pink tongue kept lapping at her hand as he settled across her legs, paws hanging off each side of her lap. He looked as though he had no intention of ever getting down. Several names went through her mind until she came to one that seemed to fit him perfectly.

"What about Chance? In honor of the beauty of second chances."

"It's perfect." He kissed her then, but it didn't last long because Chance gave them a kiss that spanned both of their chins. They broke apart, laughing.

Grey touched her right cheek with a single finger. "I love you, Cora."

She smiled, her arms full and her heart nearly bursting. "I love you, too."

THANK you so much for reading **I Still Do**. I hope you'll consider leaving a review. I Still Do was originally included in the Second Chance with You series, and is now part of the **Healing Hearts Series**. All books in this series are stand-alone and can be read in any order. Check out **Calming the Storm** for a contemporary marriage of convenience story.

WHEN I WROTE I Still Do, I knew immediately that Grey's brother, Dare, needed a story of his own. You can read it in the book **Charmed by the Daring Cowboy**:

SHE'S A LANDSCAPER ON A DEADLINE. He's a cowboy assigned to help. Will their growing attraction get in the way, or blossom into true love?

Alyssa Reid has never shied away from a challenge, but she may be in over her head this time. The single mom is juggling two landscaping projects with strict deadlines. Having her young son and an ornery runaway goat underfoot certainly isn't helping. A handsome cowboy is assigned to help her, and she finds herself losing focus in a whole new way.

Dare Jackson knows what it's like to be raised by a single mom. When the Sage Valley ranch hand meets Alyssa and her son Noah, he's immediately drawn to them. The more he gets to know them, the more he wants to be there for them both. But with every attempt he makes, he can feel Alyssa pulling farther away. He needs to change his game plan, and fast, because he's already having trouble imagining life without her.

Alyssa is afraid to trust her heart--and her son's--to the kind cowboy. Dare doesn't know how to convince her he's worth the risk. Can they meet in the middle? Or, like Hopscotch the goat, will true love escape their grasp?

Read it now!

Want a FREE BOOK?
Sign up for Melanie D. Snitker's newsletter
and get her novella, *Finding Forever*
in Romance, **FREE!**

Sign up today!

SPECIAL THANKS

Doug, I never could've finished this book without your support, tough love, and encouragement. Thank you for being there for me. You are my hero!

These last months have been anything but easy, and having a group of people who never let me give up was essential to getting this book finished. Kris, Rachel, Franky, Melissa, and Crystal, you ladies are rock stars.

Krista, I can't thank you enough for your fabulous editing skills and for being so flexible.

My wonderful beta readers are just plain awesomesauce. Thank you, Steph, Denny, and Alice, for everything. Your eagle eyes and suggestions are golden.

ABOUT THE AUTHOR

Melanie D. Snitker has enjoyed writing fiction for as long as she can remember. She started out writing episodes of cartoon shows that she wanted to see as a child and her love of writing grew from there. She and her husband live in Texas with their two children, who keep their lives full of adventure. They also have two dogs and a guinea pig who add a dash of mischief to the family dynamics. In her spare time, Melanie enjoys photography, reading, crochet, baking, and hanging out with family and friends.

https://www.melaniedsnitker.com/
https://www.facebook.com/melaniedsnitker
https://twitter.com/MelanieDSnitker
https://www.instagram.com/melaniedsnitker/